25 Servings of Soop

Stories of Emotion, Contemplation, Laughter, and Imagination

∽

Volume II

25 Servings of SOOP Volume II
Stories of Emotion, Contemplation, Laughter, and Imagination
Copyright © 2021

All rights reserved. No part of this book may be reproduced in any form whatsoever, by photography or xerography or by any other means, by broadcast or transmission, by translation into any kind of language, nor by recording electronically or otherwise without permission in writing from the author, except by a reviewer who may quote brief passages in critical articles or reviews.

ISBN 978-1-954102-03-3

Library of Congress Control Number: 2020935111
Printed in the United States of America
First Printing: 2021
18 17 16 15 14   5 4 3 2 1

Curated by Dannelle Gay
Edited by Catherine Bordeau
Interior design by Michael Grossman
Cover design by Dragan Bilic
Illustrations by Nikolin Zanati

SOMETHING OR OTHER PUBLISHING
Madison, Wisconsin 53719
Info@SOOPLLC.com
For bulk orders e-mail: Orders@SOOPLLC.com
retailers@soopllc.com

TABLE OF CONTENTS

Foreword v

Stories to Tug at Your Emotions 1

Residential – by Nancy Coleman 3

Sunshine Acres – by Natalie Wright 8

Stop to Smell the Grass – by M.D. Jerome 16

The Wishing Well – by Megan Markovic 22

Dead End Drive – by Melissa Rose Bushey 29

Men of Troy, Hoi Polloi – by Bill Cushing 36

Dying Innocence – by Ruby G. 46

Stories that Make You Think 49

Starships & Rockets – by The Poet Q 51

Thief – by Kurt Wagner 53

Envy – by Regan W. H. Macaulay 60

Admit One – by Tycho Dwelis 61

Round Midnight – by Celine Elizabeth 68

Three Friends – by E. A. Rohrmoser 75

Bend and Break – by Mary Ramsey 80

His Divine Balcony – by Madhushri Mudke 85

Stories to Make You Laugh 91

A Tough Nut to Crack – by Dannelle Fraser Gay 93

Stolen Moment – by Linné Elizabeth 99

The Recital – by Wade Fransson 106

Stories to Help You Imagine the Possibilities 111

The Ballad of Is'adora – by A.M. Mac Habee 113

Of Quests, Firefighters, and Reluctant Witches –
by J.M. Rhineheart...122

Bird on a Wire – by Kaitlyn Tovado 137

Doors Between – by Justin Attas 142

Reuben – by Regan W. H. Macaulay..148

The Will – by KristaLyn A. Vetovich 153

Shadow Reels – by Suzanne Wyles...168

v

FOREWORD

I don't know what it is about short stories that makes me want to read them. It could be the feelings they evoke, or maybe I just like being able to empathize with the characters, to step into their shoes for a little while. Either way, this book has immersed me in some of the best short stories I've ever read.

When we call to mind the best stories, they are often those that make us laugh, pull us in emotionally, perhaps making us cry, to think past the norm, and even imagine the possibilities, whether they be pleasant or scary.

25 Servings of SOOP, Volume II does just that. It is a compilation of short stories that can do all of that for you. This book features an eclectic mixture of twenty-five different authors who have written twenty-five wholly unique and original tales or poems to take your mind off of life's stresses and help you make a brief escape into their worlds. With something for everyone, this volume is sure to be loved by all readers.

I found myself transported to the fateful island that forgot to honor their gods and goddesses. I found myself imagining that fine line between politics and the person being crossed in an almost Orwellian fashion. I found myself cheering for the best of humanity—humbling as it may be. And I found myself laughing over something as silly as a squirrel's antics.

I loved being taken through the written word to different times and places around the globe and identifying with some universal themes.

If you're looking for something to devour on a rainy afternoon or the perfect gift for that hard-to-buy-for person, this gem of a book is it. This single volume, as well as its predecessor, literally has something for everyone. I hope that you enjoy these as much as I did!

Happy Reading!

Dannelle Gay
SOOP Director of Anthologies

SECTION ONE:

STORIES TO TUG AT YOUR EMOTIONS

RESIDENTIAL
NANCY COLEMAN

The first time they washed us, they scrubbed as if they would take the color right off our skin. It was cold. It would always be cold in that building at the four corners of the wind, and we stood in a line in the Girls Hall wearing nothing at all. We were all sizes, some as tall as me, some little puppies, and some of the girls held tight onto their bodies where the shape of breasts was forming. Except for Denna May, we were not my family, not even my clan, but we were all Indians, even the two women—one big and square, the other one just plain tall—who lifted us into tubs and scraped us raw. "So dirty," one said. The other one stuck her hand between my legs and rubbed *there* with a cloth. "She's beginning to smell."

The first time they washed us was also the first time I saw a mirror. It's not that I had never seen my face. Reflections in the water tell us we're not as solid as we think we are, tell us it will all change anyway, tell us that time and who we are will ripple out and find calm, and then ripple out again. Water in the lakes give us the deep brown of our skin. Trees take from the Earth through their roots and then give themselves back to her when they lie down deep in her lakes and rivers and feed her with their flesh. We are the people of oak and maple, and the sap that runs in our veins, river water when we're young, becomes syrup as we age. That's what Nimishoomis told me, why he's so sweet.

And ice. Winter ice on the lake forms so clear and deep that I can see down through many moons of storms, layers both frozen and floating. On the surface, flat swirls and ridges of stilled and silent wind. Just below, a perfect red maple leaf pauses before it turns brown and curls at the edges, holding its breath. A bit

3

Residential ～ Nancy Coleman

deeper, acorns roll and then are caught in the cold grip, another layer. I would fold onto my knees and bend low to the ice, and there, close up, and I could see the mysterious Beings that came from the depths and fell in there, ice-shadows of stories yet to be told. But in the ice, you do not see your own face.

After they scrubbed, they cut our hair. Into a chair, shears snipping away so fast—all the seasons that hair had ever seen. Cold air on my neck. And then we swept up our own feathers and threw them away. I palmed a tress of the hair of my whole life and stood up in front of a wall of little metal mirrors over metal sinks.

I was pretty, flat-faced, and round-cheeked with sparkle-eyes, which at that moment had nothing to do with how I felt. My hair stopped short and surprised beside my ears and my mouth, in a straight thin line, and looked mad.

"Proud girl, are you," Big Scrubber said from her station at the tubs. "Need to wash you again?"

I caught a glimpse of my own grin before I looked down and away.

She left me alone that time.

After they scrubbed us to clean us of the diseases we carried, after the haircuts, Big Scrubber and Tall-as-a-Tree sat us in hard chairs in straight lines in the big room across from the other big room with the dining tables. Some of us, especially the younger children, perched big-eyed and quiet. Some of us squirmed in chairs. A boy made flapping arms when the guard women weren't watching, and I laughed. He fake-frowned at me. Two very tall, very white people in long black clothes appeared in the room as quietly as the rising moon and swept to the front. The yellow-haired woman saw me laughing. She looked away through the windows at the back of the room. I had never known of laughing that didn't make other people laugh too. The room fell quiet, and I felt the cold across the back of my neck where there had once been hair.

It was 1944. We'd been speaking English when we needed to for over four generations. We understand more than we let on and more than we talk. But here, they would teach us to be Christian, and Christians speak English all the time.

The Old Ones tell us this is the age of the White People. They tell us it will not last forever. We are patient people, they say. But already on that first day, my mind was changing about becoming a Christian, and now I did not feel so patient.

And so that evening I followed my mind. I left the school for the first time—out the back door, across the dooryard, and all the way to the edge of the bluff where field flowers and three-leafed poison vines grew wild. As if I was a free person and it was an ordinary day, I kept going through the dark and through the woods that scraped at my legs and whispered their night thoughts. Big Joseph Treehorn picked me up on his drive to town in the school's truck early the next morning as I crossed the main road headed toward the sunrise. So, I thought. I learned some things.

And what did they do when I came back? Nothing. It was as if it didn't matter to them that I was there, but it mattered even less when I wasn't. If anything, the Reverends gave me less attention than they did the day before. Breakfast came and went in silence, me in my wrinkled clothes and bits of the woods in my hair and the other kids staring with question marks on their faces. We sat in class, all the kids stuffed in one room and the windows closed. Every room seemed even smaller than it had before, and I wondered if I ever would be able to breathe there.

We practiced the English language, beginning with names. After we sat down and after we stopped rustling, the blond-haired woman with the face of ice glided into the room on her black wings.

"Your names are not your names," said the Mrs. Reverend. "The names you were given are the names of things, not of people." I looked up at the high window of the room, felt the sun of the outdoors on my face. "Tree something. Rock. Animal. These are primitive names." She brought her hands to her chest, my grandmother's gesture for her heart. "We are not primitive people. We are Christians. From this day, until you are given your personal Christian name, you will take numbers."

Beginning with Forty-Seven, the hunched girl at the front of the room, we learned our number names. My name was Fifty-Three. This was hard to say, the "f" and "th" so close together they bumped into one another in my mouth, but Mrs. Reverend didn't stop me or make me say it again. She slid over me as though I was a tiny bump in the road.

Residential ～ Nancy Coleman

"Did you get away? Did you get caught?" Under the cover of the sounds of pouring and scrubbing as we washed the morning's dishes, a girl asked me in what was apparently her version of a whisper. Fifty-Two was a wide-eyed bouncing girl who skittered even when she was elbow deep in the kitchen sink. Her name should be Rabbit, I thought. And since our names come from our birth, until we are old enough to claim another, who would I be now? Who is a girl whose name is not her own? Who is a girl whose name is a number, next to all the other numbers in a straight line?

"I went walking," I said. Rabbit girl bumped against my side, hip to my thigh, and I felt something like a giggle start there and move its way up through my belly, where I tried to squeeze tight around it, to keep it to myself. But it was a giggle that wouldn't be stopped. Fifty-Two and Fifty-Three snorted almost in unison, and, at the same time, we scrubbed harder and poured more water over the rinsing dishes as we laughed through our noses. Fifty-Two bumped me again, her whole body leaning. No, not Rabbit, I thought; she's soft as a Rabbit and bounces like a Rabbit, but she's cuddly, just a Bunny in her Mama's lap rooting around for her bunny sisters.

The shadow that fell silently over us was Big Scrubber, stick in hand, hands at hips. You could tell she was Indian only in that one way—that she walked without footfall and loomed about where you least expected. Bunny Fifty-Two stiffened and scrubbed. I looked up, eyes to eyes, and didn't blink. Big Scrubber's wooden face stayed quiet, but her stick hand twitched.

There, I thought, *there*. Laughter tucked itself back down inside as I turned to the sink again. And when the blow of the stick fell across my back, buckled my knees, and dropped me to the cold floor, its burst of pain spreading through my body like an exploding star, laughter sent up its own reply, *You can't have me.*

That was all, just the one blow. When I pulled my body back upright to stand next to Fifty-Two, who had frozen at the sink, knuckles white on the wet soapstone, Big Scrubber had already moved on. I poured clear hot water over the last of the mush bowls of breakfast, and Fifty-Two dried with quick jabs of the striped dishtowel. She did not look up or lean in again. My back sent out waves of pain. I stepped back from the sink and wiped the wide slate counter. *Still here*, I thought, as each throb of pain sent a clear cold signal to my mind. A wave of sharp pain, and then a focused thought: *Next time, I will not leave alone. When Denna May is a little older.* Another wave of pain, another thought: *Bunny Fifty-Two will not fly.*

Sleep did not come that night. Even when I turned carefully in the narrow bed, my body groaned. I felt the forest floor both soft and hard, felt my fingers dig under pain and pine mulch to find the earth, the real and solid earth that would still be there next time. I would stay, I would get what I could, and I would leave. These things were clear.

That next night and for many nights to follow, when I closed my eyes, I saw the moon shining through pine trees.

∽

Nancy Coleman is a writer of songs, poetry, essays, creative nonfiction, and novels. Her full-length work, Wide Open Writing: Embrace Your Creative Genius, *was published in 2021 by Minerva Rising Press. Her essays have also been published in* The Sun, Minerva Rising, *and* Maine Voices. *She's a psychologist by day, a writer whenever she can, and a partner in the international creative community of Wide Open Writing* https://wideopenwriting.com/. *Her story in the SOOP anthology is excerpted from her most recent novel,* Laws of Nature, *in consideration for publication. She lives in Maine, where, fortunately, nature's laws cannot be ignored.*

SUNSHINE ACRES
NATALIE WRIGHT

The mailbox is still at the end of the lane, though only a few green paint patches are left on the rusted steel. It used to have a bright yellow sun, hand-painted by my mom with the words *Sunshine Acres*. An ironic name for the location of a murder.

I haven't been here for more than forty years, but I open the box like I'd just come home from work and was checking for mail. The hinges tell me "fuck off" and won't budge, but I use two hands and pull the bitch open. The metal grinds, but I prevail.

I don't know what I expected to find inside. A signed confession? An apology?

The cold steel box is empty save for spider webs and desiccated bugs. I know it's stupid, but I feel disappointed by the peeling paint, remnants of mom's attempts to create a happy life chipped away by the years. I feel disillusioned by the emptiness that greets me after so long away from the place that molded the person I became.

I get back into the rental car and make my way up the rutted dirt lane, glad that I sprung for the SUV. The rocky dirt lane would likely eat the muffler of a smaller, lower-to-the-ground car. The path climbs up a hill, then it gradually descends.

The privacy was precisely what my pa had wanted. He moved the family away from the city to escape people he deemed undesirable. To him, that meant anyone whose skin wasn't white.

He was free to be as racist as he chose and to do with his family as he wanted in this small house in a secluded valley. Isolated in a sea of alfalfa and surrounded by pastures, we lived in a prison with invisible walls.

At the top of the hill, I realize it wasn't as steep as my child-self thought it was. The lane doesn't seem as long either.

The old barn is gone, as well as most of the other outbuildings. The realtor's black SUV is parked by the garage, the only old building left other than the house.

I'm glad to see her. She has no idea what this place really is—at least for me. She has no idea that my solar plexus is coiled in a tight knot or that I can barely breathe. I take a deep breath and force myself out of the car. She's leaning against her car door, talking on her phone. My door bangs closed, and she says a hasty goodbye.

Helen the Realtor plasters on a smile filled with perfectly straight, overly white teeth. "Ms. Ezel, glad you found your way. Have any trouble finding the place? A pretty drive, though, huh?"

I don't tell her I didn't need a GPS to make my way, that I could find it in the dark with no headlights. I also omit that I had to pull over twice just to gather myself enough to drive. Instead, I simply nod. "Just beautiful," I say. I feel like the scum that's always stuck to the bottom of the drain stopper for yanking Helen out to this shithole property just so that I can get some closure. Add it to the list of things I feel guilty about. But I play my part in this charade so that Helen can play hers. "How many acres?"

She has to look at the listing sheet. I stifle an eye roll. Any idiot can look up a listing online, and even if I hadn't lived here, I'd know the acreage because I bothered to look up the property. I wonder if Helen actually makes any money from this real estate gig because she seems as useless as a Speedo in the arctic.

"One hundred twenty-one acres," Helen adds more facts I already know. "House is a two-bedroom, one bath, fourteen hundred square feet.

Seven people lived in that house. They shared the sole bathroom.

"Natural gas heat," she adds.

Does her listing reveal how the old, single-pane windows would get frost so thick you could carve your name in it? Do any of her papers say how the kids who used to live here would go to bed wearing mittens, coats, and even hats to keep from freezing?

I remain silent.

"Oh, this is interesting. The water source is a natural spring." She looks up from her paperwork. "You'd need to get that tested as part of the inspection. Without proper filtration, old springs can have toxic levels of lead and arsenic."

I've been fighting nausea, racing heart, and sweats since the mailbox. I nearly lose my breakfast at the mention of arsenic. My scared, inner eight-year-old is sure that Helen has found out about what happened here. Has found me out. Found out that I was once poor and the child of a bigot and wife abuser. And the daughter of a killer.

I must have gone paler than my natural shade of ghostly because Helen says, "Are you okay?"

I swallow the lump in my throat—years of therapy and meditation practice kick in. I remind myself to breathe. "Yeah," I lie. "I don't travel well." Another lie.

She coughs nervously. "Shall we trot down the hill and take a look inside?" The terrified child inside wants to say "No." To get back in my rental car, drive to the nearest airport, fly away, and never return. To forget I lived here and to disremember that I was their daughter.

But I'm determined to show the child inside me the birthplace of her nightmares and neuroses. I settle for a nod, and Helen smiles.

She sets off down the hill. "I did some research on the property."

I'm breaking out in a cold sweat as we walk. What history has Helen uncovered? She couldn't possibly know about what happened here, could she? I thought my family had covered our dysfunction reasonably well.

"The house has been vacant for over two years. The current owners are— get this—*both* in jail."

I raise my eyebrows. "Both, huh? For what?"

"The mister is in for beating up the misses, and the wife is in jail for selling meth." Helen chuckles. "Real nice family," she sighs. "I'm sorry in advance for what we're likely to see inside."

I don't tell Helen how, before I got clean, I'd seen a few meth houses. I know what we're likely to see, and I brace myself for it. "How long has the current family owned it?" She consults notes on her phone. I reconsider my opinion of Helen's realtor skills.

"Ten years." She looks up from her notes. "A fairly long time." Her brows crinkle. "There will be contamination clean up, and that's reflected in the low price." She goes back to her notes. "Before the lovely couple lived here, there was a sawmill." She looks around at gently rolling green hills dotted with stumps that no one bothered to grind down. "Wonder what it looked like before they removed all the trees?"

I want to tell her it was a far cry from the barren landscape she sees. I consider telling her how my industrious mother found out about a government program that gave away trees. Mom put her kids to work, and we planted hundreds of pines. If someone hadn't hacked them all down, Helen and I would be looking at a pine forest instead of bare grass and hillsides with deep erosion crevices.

I settle for a pat response. "I'm guessing it'd be a lot more attractive with trees."

Helen nods. She brightens as she says, "Hey, you could always plant some." I ignore that idea, and thankfully Helen lets it go.

She's got to know that I'm showing little enthusiasm for this property, even if I were a legit buyer. She's probably hoping to be done with the tour quickly to show me other properties and hopefully salvage a sale. The front porch is half as large as my memory recalled it. Helen struggles with the lock. Finally, she succeeds and has to give the door some shoulder to get it open. A disgusting, acrid odor of urine precedes our entry. The stench nearly curls my nose hairs.

We enter directly into a room that could be a living room but was my parent's bedroom. Their four-poster bed is gone. So too is my mother's piano. She was raised with the idea of people being well-rounded, and just because you're poor doesn't mean you should be uneducated. The piano symbolized her family and creative roots. While living here, she didn't have the opportunity to play as much as she would have liked.

The room is now filled with stacks of old magazines and newspapers. Trash is heaped on an oversized couch that sags in the middle. The windows, which once allowed plentiful light, are covered with yellowed sheets, some stained rusty red. It's dark inside, even though it's mid-morning.

Helen's nose wrinkles up. "It certainly needs a thorough cleaning." She steps gingerly and wades into the morass.

The air is dank and foul, but that's not what makes my chest feel like it's in a compression chamber. I avert my gaze and try not to look at the place where mom worked to perfect the challenging "Flight of the Bumblebee" while I played with my dolls on the floor at her side.

Helen's talking, likely telling me more about the selling points of the home. Her voice becomes like the hum of a fan, fading into the background, ignored.

Memories flood me. Stockings hung from the banister in the next room. My pa's lounger, harvest gold velvet (it was the '70s after all). The TV with the tin foil-wrapped antenna. There were good times here as well as bad, and I allow myself to remember it all. The pressure in my chest eases a bit.

Helen's voice sounds farther away, and I realize she's found her way to the kitchen. The clamps on my chest tighten back up, and my heart races. I'm standing nearly in the spot where I saw it happen. Not the killing, but the preamble to the killing.

My legs freeze. Bile rises again, and I swallow hard to keep it down. *Ghosts and shadows, Becca. It's not real,* I remind myself.

I turn toward the kitchen. There are grungy, plastic coolers piled with boxes of off-brand coffee filters, aluminum foil, and tons of empty plastic milk jugs and glass bottles. They're all stacked against the wall where he pinned her, squeezing her neck.

Darkness plays at the edges of my vision. My fisted palms are clammy. I see it in my mind's eye as plainly as if it were happening now. My eight-year-old self was the sole, silent witness to the violence. I was sure that he was going to kill her.

I can't recall what precipitated it. All I remember is sitting on a footstool, doll in hand, staring and crying. I was unable to summon the courage to stop him. I sat in fear, sure that this time he was going to end her.

My older brother had been the hero that day. He'd come in the back door and pried my pa's hands off of her. A gangly teenager and no match for my dad, but he may very well have saved her life that day.

Remembering my brother's courage, I summon enough of my own to make my way into the kitchen. Helen is quiet now, perhaps tired of talking without a response from me. I wrinkle my nose and pull my T-shirt up over my mouth and nose to keep out the stench. The smell of rotting food and garbage mixes with the chemical smell, and my head swims. Chipped glass pans caked with powdery residue are strewn across the stovetop.

There's no sheet on the back window that looks from the kitchen out to what used to be a flower garden around an old cistern. The lilac bush is still there, albeit the branches gnarled and leaves sparse. It has only scattered flowers now, not the cloud of purple it once had. It had been there when we first occupied the place nearly fifty years ago. I'm surprised it still lives.

Helen asks if I want to see the bathroom, and I shake my head. It's all I can do to keep myself from puking or passing out. I need air.

"The basement is the only other thing to see on the lower floor."

I really don't want to go down there. I don't need to see the dirt floor and dank stone walls. It had a tendency toward rats when my mother was on rat poison patrol. It's likely the rodents had built condos in her absence.

I find my tongue and tell Helen, "I think I'd like to see the backyard."

The horrific smell matches the violent crime that occurred here. Helen nods and quickly makes her way to the back door, apparently as eager as I am to be out of this malodorous house. Helen breathes deeply of the fresh air and remarks on how surprisingly lovely the backyard is. Unlike the trees that were mowed down like a stand of weeds, no one has unearthed the hundreds of bulbs and bushes my mom planted in the back. The mid-spring garden is bursting with the color of purple irises, orange tiger-lilies, and yellow jessamine. And then there's the lilac bush. Once the centerpiece of the garden, it now looks out of place. Its twisted trunk and scaly branches are a stark contrast to the verdant and showy garden happening around it.

Maybe it's just old. Or perhaps its roots have been poisoned by the body buried beneath it.

My feet walk me over to it though I don't recall telling them to. My eyeballs are hot and my breaths shallow. One minute pa sat in his chair at the kitchen table, drinking his morning coffee. The next minute his face went pale, and he let out a gurgling gasp. Within seconds there was a loud thud as he fell out of the chair. He lay on the vinyl floor, drooling and gasping, his legs twitching.

My mom had screamed and dropped a cast-iron pan of bacon she'd been draining of the grease. She never complained about the burns on her legs from that. An older brother had come running at the sound of her scream and, a few minutes later, my older sisters, too. One of them gave him mouth-to-mouth, and another called in the emergency. There was crying and shouting and questions to my mom about what had happened. Sobbing hysterically, my mom had been little help. No one bothered to ask me. I guess they figured an eight-year-old doesn't know anything.

But I did know. I'd seen mom pour an odd powder into his coffee before he'd even entered the room. She hummed a hymn as she stirred it, oblivious to the fact that I was there, as I usually was, playing quietly at her feet, ignored. Unseen, I soaked it all up like a thirsty sponge—a witness to too much.

No one asked me what I'd seen. I guess there was no need. The arsenic was odorless, and pa's death was recorded as a heart attack. They handed his ashes to the grieving widow, and she buried them in the garden where I stand.

We moved away not long after his death. I'd been joyous to be rid of the place. In many ways, my life began where and when his ended.

I stand beside the lilac bush where my greatest secret is buried. I heave out great sobs, no longer guarding myself or caring what Helen may think of me.

I'm not crying for him because, to this day, I'm sure that karma's a bitch, and she served up exactly what he'd ordered. I don't cry for mom either. In the end, the cancer of what she'd done ate her alive. She paid for her crime, just not in the way that society prefers a person to pay.

The slightly rotten smell of the lilacs matches my mood. I grieve the premature death of my childhood. I chose neither the dysfunction nor being witness to a murder. *But you did choose to stay silent.* A voice within me reminds me.

I take a deep breath and let my guilt over that go. He was dead. Her rotting in jail would have helped no one. My silence may have been selfish, but it came from a primordial survival instinct that resides within us all.

There's a warm hand on my arm. I'd forgotten Helen was there.

"Are you okay?"

I nod and sniffle. Helen hands me a tissue.

"You lived here."

It isn't a question. I nod again.

She doesn't ask me any more questions, and I'm grateful. Helen stands with me as I bury my guilt beneath the lilac bush, beside the ashes of the father my mother killed.

∽

Natalie writes speculative fiction short stories and novels, including the award-winning H.A.L.F. trilogy. She is also a podcaster and co-host of The Tipsy Nerds Bookclub (The best of science fiction and fantasy—with a twist), and a frequent panelist at comic-cons and book festivals. She is currently wrangling a new epic fantasy novel in a planned five-book series. When not writing, reading, or editing, Natalie enjoys international travel, cooking French food, and playing MMORPGs. She lives in Arizona with her husband, daughter, and two cat overlords.

STOP TO SMELL THE GRASS
M.D. JEROME

It was Saturday. A crisp spring night awaited outside Xavier Owen's window while he sat atop his bed aimlessly scrolling Twitter. Outside really wasn't an option these days.

They were *still* in quarantine, the coronavirus spiking as March came to a close. Now, it was April, and classes were still closed, with finals on the horizon. He had no idea when he'd be able to return home.

When the virus broke out, Xavier's first thoughts were of home, an idea that was quickly obliterated after one phone call to Wales. His grandparents lived with his parents. He couldn't risk travel, only to come home and put a family member at risk. It was safer, his mum had said, for him to stay put in Canada in the apartment he was renting close to his university, especially since his student visa was still valid. Luckily, thanks to his parents, he had rent money, so there was a roof over his head. He was safe and healthy. There were a lot of people in a similar situation, but some people had it worse. At least he wasn't alone, and, as if on cue, like his roommate knew he had the spotlight, J. Cole's "No Role Modelz" began blasting. The beat of the base caused the frames hanging on Xavier's wall to rattle.

Xavier's roommate, J.S. Woods, wouldn't have been his choice for sharing quarantine. He'd have preferred his mum and her home-cooked meals or even his long-time girlfriend, who had left campus and driven back to Brampton to stay with her family.

Xavier and J.S. had become friends after spending the majority of the school year living together. J.S. was his polar opposite, the literal north

16

to his south. He was brass and blunt, and, like an adrenaline junkie, he always sought out a new challenge. He was messy and loud, preferring to amend the rules versus following them, whereas Xavier had always been quiet and shy with a small dose of OCD. He was often uncertain and hesitant, a complete rule-follower, which was why people like J.S. scared the living crap out of him. It was like being forced to ride a roller coaster ... blindfolded.

No, his roommate J.S. definitely wasn't who he'd have picked to be, *literally*, the sole individual he could have physical contact with during quarantine. However, because they *were* each other's sole contact, they'd become best friends. Hell, Xavier would even go as far as to call J.S. the brother he never had. A pandemic causes a different way of thinking.

Again, as if on cue, J.S. opened Xavier's bedroom door—without knocking as was his way. "Yo, you wanna go on a walk?" he shouted over the blare of Kanye West's "Champion."

"Sure, I got nothing better to do." Xavier got off the bed, tucking his phone in his pocket.

"Cool."

Together they walked down the hall and put their sneakers on. Gray plastic gloves were stretched over their hands. Face masks that J.S. had illustrated in vibrant colors were adjusted over their mouths and noses, something they did now without thinking. It was as mundane as tying shoelaces. This was the new norm for who knew how long.

"You going to shut off the music?" Xavier inquired.

"Nah, the Bluetooth will just disconnect as we get farther."

J.S.'s way of thinking always confused Xavier. "Or you could just turn it off now..."

"Nope," he answered with a pop of his mouth. "Come on."

When they made it out of their building, they walked together in silence, allowing the cool air to wash over them. Thankfully, it wasn't snowing, but the wind held a bite burning the tops of J.S.'s ears. The sky remained free of a single cloud, and the ground was dry.

"Fresh air isn't something I'll ever take for granted again," J.S. muttered.

Stop to Smell the Grass ❧ M.D. Jerome

"I know what you mean. It's all we got."

"Literally."

"Hey, how's your family doing?" Xavier asked J.S., who was stranded like him. That was discovered after he had packed up and was ready to head home when he learned that one of his family members who lived in the same community as his folks had contracted the virus. His father had determined that it would be better for everyone to just stay put.

"Good, good. My uncle and aunt seem to be on the tail-end of it. They're assuming my aunt, who went on a work trip, was the source," answered J.S.

"That's crazy, man." The whole world was losing its mind about the virus, and every new finding, stat, or fact Xavier read always produced the same comment: "This is crazy." It was wild history in the making. Future articles would read: "When the World Temporarily Shut Down." He pondered the disheveled state humanity would be in once it emerged from the pandemic. He wasn't thinking about economics or financial declines, but the essence of humans forced to be contained and contactless. What would the aftermath look like?

"So, are you going to go back home then?" asked J.S. He tried to keep the horror of being quarantined by himself out of his voice. He realized that they'd become each other's rock without knowing it.

"Nah, my mom said it's better if I stay where I am. Especially since you and I have been quarantined from the start. It makes sense."

"Ya, I know what you mean." J.S. hoped that his nonchalant tone camouflaged his relief.

"Your parents—they're good?"

"Ya, no change there. They aren't taking any risks, especially with my grandparents."

"Crazy times," Xavier whispered. "Crazy times."

They continued aimlessly, wandering until they reached the soccer field. It was an impressive field despite it being the location where the Toronto Varsity Blues practiced. Xavier watched as J.S. walked over to the locked gate and rattled it.

"It's locked, dummy," he said with a laugh.

"I know that, but the fence doesn't look that high…" J.S. drifted off as he looked over at him with a gleam in his eyes. Xavier knew that look and knew that behind the mask there was a mischievous smile to match.

"Oh, no way!"

"Coooooome on!" J.S. whined, turning from the locked fence toward him.

"We don't even have a ball!" Xavier countered.

"I bet you inside that hut," replied J.S. pointing to a large hut painted University of Toronto blue, "is where they store all the balls."

"This is ridiculous. It's obviously locked for a reason."

"It's either this or burning down a church. Come on, my soul is dying! We only go to the grocery store and back home again. We don't go anywhere else. We're following all the rules. But I gotta be honest, I'm losing it a little."

"And this will help?" Xavier questioned skeptically, rolling his eyes at J.S.'s dramatics.

"Yes! Just some fun one-on-one competition. Best out of three, and then we'll turn right back home."

"I don't know…" started Xavier, and J.S. knew he was winning the battle as Xavier's eyes lit up a bit. But Xavier protested, "What if we get caught?"

"Need I remind you that we're in a pandemic? The authorities have bigger fish to fry than some uni students playing soccer at their *own* school."

"On a locked-up field!" Xavier cut in.

"Come on, you know you're doing it. Let's go. I'll give you a boost." J.S. didn't say anything else. He turned back to the gate and bent down; his hand was propped and ready to boost Xavier up. On a sigh, he went. Of course, he did. J.S. gave him the boost and then climbed up and over after him. They walked over to the hut, and J.S. had been right. There were a handful of soccer balls in a bag. Lucky for them, there was one that wasn't flat.

"I'm surprised they left it unlocked," Xavier thought out loud.

"Ya, me too. I was worried I'd have to pick the lock."

Xavier rolled his eyes at his friend, who, of course, knew how to pick a lock. "Maybe with how fast everything happened, they forgot to lock it."

Stop to Smell the Grass ∽ M.D. Jerome

"Ya, probably. All right, UK man, let's see those soccer moves!" J.S. challenged, tossing the ball in Xavier's direction. "What do you call it... Football?" he inquired with a terrible English accent.

"I do *not* sound like that!" Xavier hollered out as he began treading up the field with the ball.

They played using most of the field, and Xavier realized that he hadn't laughed so hard in a long time. The workings of the universe, he often found, were ironic. Two distinctly opposite people were forced together during a pandemic. Due to extenuating circumstances, they'd been required to be each other's constant human connection, something he believed that humans were unable to live without.

After J.S. scored on Xavier, he walked back with the ball, and Xavier said to him: "This is great! I know it sounds lame but, I don't know, my..."

"...Soul feels lighter?" J.S. finished for him with a raise of his brow.

It was sheepish, really, guys talking about souls and stuff, but there wasn't any other way to phrase how he felt. "Ya," he nodded.

Sometimes people were placed in your life for a reason. When everything felt dark, sometimes an outrageous friend could push you outside of your comfort zone to see the good again. The pandemic was teaching him a new way of life. His quarantine buddy was teaching him not to take things for granted. Something as simple as a soccer ball and grass could make him hope for a world where the stadiums would be full again while players competed on the field. He hoped for a world where they emerged from all of this better for the experience.

* * *

"Check that out," his partner's soft voice said in his direction.

Officer Simpson kept his eyes on the road and his ears perked for any updates coming over the police scanner. When he turned to see what his partner was pointing to, he was pleasantly shocked.

"They're... playing soccer?"

"Ya," his partner said, also dumbfounded. "Should we go in?"

He thought it through for a second before briefly glancing at the boys again. One cheered as he scored on his friend, doing a ridiculous victory dance across the field.

"No," he answered, the boys tugging a smile from his mouth. "Let them have their fun."

M.D. Jerome is enjoying her twenties and living with her fiance and their dog. She was born and raised in Toronto, relocated to Houston, and currently resides in Nova Scotia. She graduated with honors and received a BA in English Literature in 2017 from the University of Toronto. She is an avid reader with no qualms about being a writer until 2014, when she woke from a vivid dream and decided to give it a shot. You can find her on Twitter: @mdjerome_. Or chat with her via email: m.d.jeromewriter@gmail.com.

THE WISHING WELL
MEGAN MARKOVIC

*D*eep in the forest, down a long-wooded path, next to an old oak tree, lies a wishing well that anyone can see. People walk from miles away just to get a peep. Not many persons make their wishes for, you know, you only get one chance next to that old oak tree.

Something woke her up earlier than usual that morning. Turning around to untangle her sheets from a whole night of dreams, she reached out for him. *Still just a dream*, she thought with disappointment, as she closed her eyes. She was hoping to get one more look at him before she started her day. Then, there he was with his strong blue eyes staring back at her. Taking a quick screenshot and storing it away in the little box that belonged to him in her brain, as she slowly sat up, rubbed her eyes, and swung her legs around the bed. Her tired feet hit the floor as she stood, memories rushing to her head. "Twenty seconds," she said to herself. Yesterday was forty. Her record was forty-five. Forty-five seconds until the memories of him rushed through her mind. Some days the memories lifted her up and gave her peace. Other days they weighed her down with extreme sadness, the type of sadness that made her want to stay in bed with the shades down and sleep the day away. She had learned months ago that sleep was the only time she was happy because it was only then that she saw him.

Slowly walking down the stairs, she listened to the creaking of the old wooden steps with every step she took. They drowned out the noise in her head as she savored every step each morning, day after day, month after month. When she reached the kitchen, she would fill up her coffee maker with water and stare out the window, waiting.

She thought of him standing next to her in his kitchen, picking her up and setting her on the counter to passionately kiss her. Then she wondered if he had ever finished rebuilding his deck. What did it look like now? She wondered who helped him and wished she was sitting next to him, drinking coffee in the cool morning shade, Tom Petty playing in the background as their feet intertwined on the big lounge chair he'd bought for them to share. This is how her mind worked now. One small thought of him spiraled into a whole day of obsessing, wondering, wishing, hoping, and dreaming. For weeks her friends had been telling her to snap out of it. To move on. But that's not how love works. Especially this love—her love for him.

When her coffee finished brewing, she filled her favorite mermaid mug, leaving just enough room for a shot of whiskey. *I'm doing pretty good so far*, she thought. Some mornings she skipped the coffee altogether and went straight for the whiskey. She sat down, sipping her coffee and savoring every moment, thinking of them together on his deck.

Finally, when she had drunk the last drop, she headed back up her creaky steps to her bedroom. "Seven o'clock in the morning," she said out loud, "Just enough time to go back to my dreams." She crawled back under her covers, throwing her legs around in the air until the covers were under them, rolled onto her side, and fell fast asleep.

There they were, sitting under the willow tree, holding hands and looking out on the lake. He was talking and she was mesmerized, not by his words but by how his lips moved when he spoke and how he laughed from deep in his soul. She sat there, smiling at him, thinking how lucky she was.

Finally, when he was done talking, he leaned in and kissed her. She loved his soft lips. She could kiss those lips for a lifetime. As he pulled away, she opened her eyes, no longer sitting next to him at the lake. Now, she was in his house, sitting in his reclining chair. This was her favorite spot in his home. She would sit here for hours while reading, next to the big picture window. It was a magical chair next to a magical window. They always brought her peace, made her feel at home.

Suddenly, she heard a faint voice coming from outside. She sat up from the chair and followed the voice through the kitchen. When she reached the back door, the voice was louder. *The wishing well, the wishing well*, it repeated over and over, like a child's whisper in her ear. She opened the door and stepped outside. Now she was in the forest and the whisper was all around her, *the wishing well, follow me to the wishing well.* Over and over the voice repeated itself, making her head spin. Soon the trees were spinning around her, and the voice was getting louder and louder. From a whisper to a scream: *COME TO THE WISHING WELL.*

She was jolted back to consciousness, sweat dripping down her face. Looking around her bedroom, she slowly woke up and realized that this wasn't just another dream. This was a sign! A sign she had been looking for—for months. "It's time," she said out loud.

One second, she thought after jumping out of bed. As the memories rushed to her, she shook her head as if to shake them away like a dog shakes water off its back. She ran over to her dresser and opened her smooth, wooden jewelry box. She picked up the coin and rubbed its center with her thumb, closed her eyes, and remembered the night he gave her this coin.

They had been at the fair, him playing games and her arms full with an array of stuffed animals he had won for her. When they had no more arms to carry the stuffed creatures, they headed toward the exit. A big sign was lit up: "Fortunes Told Here. May All Your Dreams Come True." She laughed, thinking how hokey that sounded, but he walked right over and handed the woman a twenty-dollar bill and sat down. She stood back, trying not to listen to the fortune being told. As he said goodbye to the fortune teller, she whispered something in his ear while putting something in his hand. Then looked over at her and winked. When they got to the exit, he leaned down and kissed her, putting the fortune teller's gift in her hand. She looked down and saw a shiny penny with a butterfly cut out of the center. She smiled and said, "Well, isn't that ironic?"

He looked at her and said, "I'd say it's fate." Butterflies were their thing—kind of like a secret club between the two of them.

She shook the memory out of her head, dropped the coin in her pocket, and rushed toward the staircase. This time, though, she didn't savor every step but ran down them as fast as she could, grabbed her keys off the table, and ran out the door. Nervous excitement was building up in her as she drove to the forest. She had been waiting for this moment for months. She had never been undecided about the wishing well. However, you only get one wish in a lifetime, so her friends had made her promise to wait, to make sure what she wanted was true and real. After all, she had a whole lifetime ahead of her. How could she use up her one wish now? But even though she knew one million percent what she wanted, she had obliged her friends anyway.

She drove down the winding road along the river, and, at every bend, a new memory flashed in her head. About halfway to the forest, she realized that she had forgotten her shoes in the rush of leaving the house. She laughed, thinking, *There's no way I'm turning around for them now.*

When she arrived at the forest, she parked her car on the roadside and quietly exited her vehicle. She checked her pocket to ensure that the coin was safe and slowly walked toward the path. When she arrived at the path entrance, she rubbed her hand over the rock containing the Wishing Well rules. There were four simple rules that she read slowly to herself:

You must walk the path quietly, for my wishes don't like to be disturbed.

When you arrive at my home, close your eyes, drop your coin, and make your wish.

Remember, ONE wish in a lifetime.

NEVER wish out loud.

When she finished reading each word, she took a step toward the path, then another and another, looking at her feet as she walked. Feeling each woodchip piercing the bottoms of her feet reminded her she that didn't have shoes on. She stopped to take a break, holding back tears from the pain. She could feel the blood oozing from her heels but didn't dare look at them out of fear that it would slow her down. She took a deep breath and kept moving. *I will crawl if I must*, she thought. To take her mind off the pain, she looked forward up the path and noticed how dark it was. It was only two o'clock in the afternoon, but it looked like dusk. She was rubbing her eyes to help them adjust to the darkness when all of a sudden fireflies lit up around her, lighting her way. Then, she noticed the path was lined with giant willow trees, their beautiful branches swaying in the wind over the path. It was almost like they were guiding her way, calling her toward the well.

She also saw beautiful blue flowers that part of her thought weren't real. They were the size of her head and looked like a plumeria mated with a Gerber daisy. Their leaves were bright green, and they seemed to move with her. Every step she took, they followed alongside her. If she hadn't been in such a hurry to get to the well, she would have stopped to investigate them. She saw birds, squirrels, and even deer, everything you'd expect to see in a forest. One thing she noticed, though, was that the atmosphere was silent. Even the wind didn't make a noise as if it, too, knew the rules of the wishing well. Wishes don't like to be disturbed!

The path ended at a wide circle with the old oak tree in the middle. Staring at it, she took a deep breath and let her eyes wander to the well. There it was. She was expecting something magical. *Maybe the well will sparkle, or light will shine on it from the heavens*, she had thought for months. But no, this was just an average well, built with stone, with moss and mold growing all over it. She shook off the wave of disappointment that had slowly crept over her and took a step toward it. Then another and another until her feet were almost touching its stones. She stood there staring at it and taking a screenshot in her mind. Slowly, she reached into her pocket for the coin. Rubbing its center with her thumb, like she had done so many times before, she said goodbye to a treasure. Finally, she pulled the coin out of her pocket, kissed it, and held it over the well, slowly closing her eyes and concentrating on her wish. She opened the palm of her hand, letting her fingers fly into the air, dropping the coin into its new home. Then, quietly in her head, she made her wish.

Afterward, with her eyes still closed, she leaned over the well and waited to hear her beloved coin hit bottom. She heard nothing. Not even a rustling of a tree. She opened her eyes and felt disoriented. Had she been daydreaming? Had she walked away from the well and not realized it? Panic overcame her until she noticed the oak tree and saw where the wishing well had once sat. "Well, there's the magic I was looking for," she said to herself with a smile. She turned around to head back down the path. This time, though, the path was different. The wood chips and flowers were gone and the trees were no longer lining the way. It was now just a small dirt path, the size of someone's bicycle tires with long grass growing over it. She ran. The dirt mixing with the blood left a cushion feeling on the soles of her feet. She ran and ran and ran until the path ended and she was back at the entrance. She looked around for the stone. It had disappeared, too. "They're serious on that one wish rule, huh?" she said to herself.

She took one last look at the forest and walked to her car. As she drove back down the winding river road, she couldn't help but miss her coin. It was one of her most favorite gifts, which was why it went into the wishing well, of course. She was going to miss rubbing her thumb over the opening in the center. But the benefits of giving up the coin far outweighed keeping it. When she arrived home, she walked up her creaky wooden steps and rounded the corner to her bathroom. She turned the water on in the tub and slowly set each of her aching feet inside it. She laid her head against the wall and pictured her coin falling down the well and her wish coming true.

When she finished caring for her feet, she crawled into bed, ready to go back to her dreams. This time, however, she couldn't fall asleep. She tossed and turned until, at last, she threw the covers off and got up.

She puttered around the house for about an hour, coffee and whiskey in hand, until she decided she'd had enough. It was only six o'clock in the evening, so she grabbed her book and hopped into the car. Before pulling down the driveway, she looked down at her bare feet and laughed. She drove the country roads with the windows down, taking in the cool September breeze. She could smell the remnants of grass cut earlier that day. Everything looked yellow with hints of green as it does in September in the Midwest. Arriving at the park, she picked up her book and headed for a picnic table. She had been here many times before, often with him and a bottle of wine to watch the sunset. After him, she would go alone. She spent almost every free night she had at this spot reading, writing, and watching the sunset. Mostly, though, she came there waiting for him. Day after day, sunset after sunset, she waited. The sound of every car that pulled in gave her a wave of excitement until she turned around and looked. Then sheer sadness and disappointment would fall over her when she realized it was just some teenagers coming to get drunk or an old man and his dog heading down the path to go fishing. Months and months of this scenario passed by, and still she never lost hope.

She opened her book and began reading. Before she knew it, the sun was setting. She turned around in her seat to watch it in all its glory. She had always thought that sunsets were beautiful, and even more so now because a sunset meant she had survived another day. She stood up to take a screenshot to store in the little box that belonged to him in her brain.

As she turned around, she felt something hit the top of her head. She looked up and thought, *Surely, that wasn't rain.* She shrugged her shoulders, and as she took a step forward, she noticed something shiny in the grass near her feet. She bent down, pushing the grass aside, and picked it up. It felt familiar. As she brought it closer to her eyes, she realized what it was. She rubbed its center with her thumb like she always had. *How could it be?* she thought. She clutched it with her hands and walked toward her car, a weird confusion rushing over her. Then she realized she had forgotten her book at the picnic table. Slowly walking back, she focused on her most prized possession back in her hands.

Then she heard a voice say, "I think this belongs to you." She looked up and there he was, smiling back at her.

∽

Megan lives in the Chicago area with her dad, fifteen-year-old son, and two golden retrievers. In her free time, she enjoys being with family and friends, writing, White Sox games and occasionally drinking too much tequila. This is her first published work. You can find her on Instagram at Megmarko83.

DEAD END DRIVE
MELISSA ROSE BUSHEY

John and Izzy had been having issues with their marriage, so John decided to surprise his wife with a getaway to their other home in Vermont. It was a secluded mountain house with a creek running behind it. It was Izzy's favorite place in the world.

They piled into the car, and she asked where they were going. He told her that it was a surprise, but she had a feeling she knew where they were going.

"This is a surprise," she smiled, knowing exactly where they were going because he drove the familiar winding roads to the house.

"I know we needed to get away," John said as he squeezed her hand.

She looked at herself in the mirror and thought to herself, "I've still got it."

They arrived at the house as the sun was setting. Izzy loved the way the house looked when the sun was going down. The mountains would glow a certain way, reflecting on the water. John grabbed the bags and walked inside the cottage. Izzy decided to go around to the back to feel the sun's warmth and look at the beautiful scenery. She took a deep breath and exhaled the fresh, pine air, and then jumped as she felt an arm around her waist.

"I didn't mean to scare you," said her husband as he handed her a glass of champagne.

"What is this for?"

"To us." She smiled at him and took a sip of the sweet champagne. "I'll never get over how the sun sets here. It makes the mountains look golden."

"I was thinking the same thing," Izzy said.

"Come on, let's have some dinner."

Dead End Drive ∾ Melissa Rose Bushey

John grabbed her hand, led her into the den, and told her to sit down. As he took her shoes off, Izzy noticed that the fireplace was burning. It felt so cozy. He walked away, and she sat there taking everything in, remembering the last time they were here. She was in deep thought when John brought her a glass of wine.

"Are you all right?"

"Yeah, I'm fine." She smiled as she took the glass.

John smiled back at her. "Dinner will be ready soon." Izzy took a sip of wine and placed it on the coffee table as she started thinking again about the last time she was here—and the fight that had almost broken up their marriage. She'd discovered that he was fooling around with his assistant from work. She'd wanted to leave him, but he'd pleaded for her to stay. It took her a while to trust him again.

Izzy thought about their two children who had grown up here on summer vacations. She remembered John showing Kate and Chris how to fish and the way Kate screamed when she saw a fish on the end of the hook. John had had to throw it back in the lake.

John pulled her back to earth when he touched her shoulder. "You look like you're deep in thought."

"I was just thinking of the time when you were showing the kids how to fish."

John started to laugh. "Oh yeah, Kate hated that."

"Yes, she did."

"Come on, dinner is ready." She got up and walked into the kitchen and saw a spread laid out before her.

"Wow, I have to admit, I'm impressed." Izzy grabbed a plate, put a little of each tempting dish on it, and sat down at the table. They started to eat, and the wine was beginning to make Izzy relax. "I'm thrilled you did this, John."

"I'm happy that you're happy."

After dinner they relaxed by the fire, made love, and fell asleep. Izzy woke up when she heard the grandfather clock chime twice. It was two in the morning. She reached her arms out for John, but he wasn't there. She wrapped the blanket around her and called out his name. There was no answer. She went into the bedroom thinking that maybe his back was hurting and he had crawled into bed, but he wasn't there. She called his name again, and yet again there was no answer.

Izzy checked the bathroom and the kitchen, to no avail. She thought she heard voices, but she didn't see anyone. So, she grabbed her robe from the bathroom, threw it on, and looked through the window. It was pitch dark outside. Even so, she opened the front door to go outside because maybe he was outside somewhere.

The chill in the air seemed to enhance the darkness. Izzy felt her way to the back of the house and didn't see him, but she did hear a noise coming from the garage area. She made her way back to the front of the house and looked through the garage window. There he was!

Only, he wasn't alone. He was with her! That woman he had had that affair with about a year ago! Her dress was hiked up, and he was inside her on the car roof. Izzy stood frozen for a moment, but then came to her senses as tears welled up. She put her hand over her mouth and stumbled backward, falling over something and landing with a thud.

When Izzy came to, she was on her bed in the bedroom. Was it all a dream? After making her way to the bathroom, she looked at herself in the mirror and felt a bump on the back of her head. Her feet were dirty from walking outside. "That wasn't a dream; that really happened," she muttered to herself. She opened the bathroom door and quietly tiptoed to the den. She wanted to grab her cell phone that she had left in her bag under the chair she had been sitting in earlier. She was about to bend down and grab it when an arm came around her waist.

"Hey, baby, what are you doing?"

"What am I doing? I saw you!"

"Saw me what?"

"You were with that woman."

"Honey, I think you had a bad dream."

"No, I don't think so," Izzy declared as she scrambled away from him and started backing slowly to the kitchen. Then she hit something. Turning around, Izzy saw that it was her—the other woman.

Dead End Drive ∽ Melissa Rose Bushey

"Sam, I told you to wait outside."

"No chance in hell, Johnny." Izzy had no idea what was happening. She looked at the woman with hatred as she pushed her away.

"What are you doing in my house?" Izzy yelled. Sam looked at John, and John looked at Izzy. He grabbed her arms and forced them behind her back. "What are you doing, John?"

"Something I should've done a long time ago." He tied her hands behind her back and put her in the chair. Izzy started to cry and scream.

Sam walked over to Izzy and slapped her in the face. "Quiet!" John went to the kitchen, found what he was looking for, and walked back into the den. He placed duct tape over her mouth. John looked at Sam and smiled. He grabbed her and held her in his arms and kissed her. "We can finally be together," she cooed. Izzy looked away from them, tears streaming down her cheeks. She couldn't believe this was happening to her. John and Sam walked into the kitchen.

"What are we going to do with her?" he asked Sam.

"If you had slipped her the sleeping pills like you were supposed to, this wouldn't be happening. Now, we have to figure out something else. Maybe we can drown her in the bathtub?"

"How would that work?"

"I don't know; you're the doctor. Don't you keep anything on you in case of emergencies?"

Meanwhile, Izzy's heart was pounding. She heard them talking about drowning her! How could this be happening? She heard them leave the kitchen and walk outside and knew that this was her only chance. She remembered her purse under the chair and wondered if she could get it without them knowing. She stood up and bent down backwards so she could feel for her bag. She was trying to grab it when she heard them coming back. She fumbled to find the strap, and, finally, she got her fingers on it. She stood up and sat back down with the bag behind her. Just then, they walked back into the den.

"You should've left me when you had the chance, Izzy." Izzy tried to talk, but she couldn't because of the tape. John pulled it off.

32

"If that's what you want, then that's fine," Izzy screamed. "If you want to be with her, then go ahead. Just don't kill me. Think about Kate and Chris." She knew that mentioning their names would get into his head.

Sam looked at John, "Don't play into that BS, John! We have to get rid of her!"

He looked at Sam with steely eyes, "Go into the kitchen!" She started to say something, but he yelled for her to go. Off she stomped into the kitchen.

"Why are you doing this?" Izzy pleaded hoarsely.

"You would never have let me go, Izzy, and we both know that I love her and we want to be together."

"Killing me is not going to help anything," she sputtered. While John had paced around while talking, she had frantically rummaged through her bag for the knife she carried when they went on hikes. Her trembling fingers had found it and tried to open it.

"Now, listen to me, you're going to have to behave. I have to go back and talk to Sam." John placed the tape back over her mouth and walked away, giving Izzy the opportunity to open the knife and adjust it to where she could cut the rope. She started sawing back and forth, and the rope was loosening.

Izzy could hear moaning coming from the kitchen. She wanted to block out everything that she was hearing. She had been married to this man for thirty years and thought she'd known everything about him. Not so. Turns out he was someone completely different than she'd realized. She managed to finally get the ropes off her wrists, got her phone, and dialed 911. leaving the line open. She could hear John or Sam coming, so she acted like she was still tied up. But the knife was in her hand, ready for use.

Then she noticed a shadow in the doorway between the kitchen and living room where she sat, pretending to still be tied up and helpless. It was the woman, Sam.

"We've decided what we're going to do with you," Sam smirked as she approached. She pulled Izzy's hair to pull her up, and Izzy started to scream. Her free hands burst forward, and she thrust the knife into Sam's neck. Sam lurched backward, looked at Izzy with dazed eyes, and fell down. Sam pulled the knife out of her neck, and blood squirted all over the floor. Sam's eyes rolled into the back of her head. Izzy didn't waste any time. She ran from the den to the hallway, away from the kitchen.

Izzy heard John walk into the den, "Oh my god, Sam." He picked up her head and pushed the hair from her eyes. He knew she was gone. He placed her head back down and got up slowly. "Izzy, where are you?"

She didn't respond. He started walking through the house to find her, but she was under the bed. He walked into their bedroom and yelled out, "Izzy, Izzy," but no answer. He opened the closet doors, but she wasn't in the closet, of course. He stood there for a moment thinking about where she could be hiding.

Izzy could see his feet walking around the room, and she lay there trying not to breathe as he moved backwards closer to the bed, his feet pointing away from her. She could hear him mumbling, "I'm going to kill that bitch." Those words burned into Izzy, and a raging instinct for survival overwhelmed her.

Izzy tightened her grip on the now-bloody knife and sliced his Achilles tendon on one ankle. He immediately fell down, screaming. She quickly came out from under the bed and stood over him. He tried to reach for her, and she kicked at his hands, but he was able to grab her leg and pull her down. John rolled on top of Izzy and started to choke her. She had dropped the knife on the way down.

As Izzy struggled to breathe, she looked around frantically for the knife. At last, she saw it and reached for it. She was running out of oxygen. Panic was setting in. She extended her arm as much as she could, reaching for the knife. Finally, she felt the cold metal, slippery with blood, in her hand. She grabbed it and jabbed the blade right into his neck. He immediately let go of *her* neck and covered *his* neck with his hands before collapsing onto her.

Izzy coughed and struggled to push John off her. After tremendous effort, she was able to get out from under him and stand up to see him lying in a pool of his own blood. She staggered into the den and saw Sam still lying there in a pool of her own blood.

Izzy was crying hysterically when she heard the door being broken down. She looked up. The police!

∾

Melissa Bushey is an avid reader. When she was little, she loved writing poetry, and that turned into short stories. She gets her inspiration from her favorite author, Stephen King, and currently has three self-published young adult fiction novels available on Amazon. She also loves doing crossword puzzles, sudoku, and yoga. Melissa lives in the suburbs of Bucks County, PA with her husband and her fur babies. She has two dogs and four cats. When she isn't with her fur babies or doing one of her many hobbies, she is working on her latest novel or short story.

MEN OF TROY, HOI POLLOI
BILL CUSHING

It is a little-known fact that King Priam of Troy, after fighting with King Menelaus of Sparta and both having laid down a coat of carnage with no measurable progress toward victory for either side, asked his son Paris—the prince whose infatuation with Helen had started war—to meet with his generals and confer what the Trojans should do next.

As did Menelaus with the Spartans.

But this is not their story.

Nor is it one of the generals, nor of the "heroes" of the war.

Instead, this is for the foot soldiers—the artisans, bakers, craftsmen, bronze smiths, potters, even philosophers—forced from their homes and pressed into defending the honor of Troy and of Paris.

Ten years in, the war had not been going well for either side, what with the lack of interference from the gods and goddesses. Even now, the immortals on Mount Olympus took advantage of the present stalemate to lay down more bets on the outcome. But let us return to our true protagonists: these "volunteers" who served, mostly to avoid the ostracism certain to befall any man who might refuse the honor.

Inside Troy's walls, the assembled troops sat with crossed legs and aching, bent backs. They had arranged themselves into small circles at first. As more men joined in, the gatherings became pockets of circles that grew and merged, eventually spiraling outward, looking like a beached nautilus to the guards trying to stay alert while standing watch in the parapets.

Kimon was a plasterer who lived at the northernmost section of Troy in the shadow of the citadel, so it only made sense that he would end up at the most inconvenient spot possible. He found himself stationed at the southern end of the city, right by Lion's Gate, as far as he could get. Not that it mattered much because even married men were allowed to spend only one day a month at home. Joining the others, Kimon watched the men sitting on the ground all around him. They ate as well as they could, gnawing on strips of salted lamb, feta cheese, and—for those who had brought *skeins*—drinking water. Trapped inside the walls for as long as they had been, supplies were short. Rations were the order of the day, every day. Meanwhile the hunger gnawing at their stomachs made many of them increasingly discontent. The war had dragged on longer than any had expected—and certainly longer than the kings and generals had promised.

"All this for some lovers' spat," Kimon muttered, more to himself than those on either side of him. "Seems a royal waste of time."

"And energy," the man to his left added.

"And lives," chimed in a third, adding, "Mostly ours."

Kimon didn't know all his compatriots' names, the men having long since gotten blended and mixed into one massive mess of infantry. He did know the next speaker, Tychon, a clothier of little note and an alchemist of even less success.

"Wasting time," Tychon mumbled as he tore into a slab of cured lamb with his remaining teeth. "That's what royalty always does best."

"Too true," replied one of the unknown men. "In fact, this war has been all waste and nothing but waste."

"*Scatta!*" Tychon chimed in. "The whole thing. One big mountain of shit."

Now the one to Kimon's immediate left spoke again, this time in righteous anger.

"Watch yourselves," he reprimanded, turning to face Kimon and revealing a deep scar running down the left side of his face, like a fork of lightning interrupted only by a crude eye patch. Clearly, he was a veteran, perhaps even a warrior.

"Besides," he said, his shoulders dropping to a more relaxed posture. "We do not question our king. We fight to defend the honor of Helen, the object of Paris's attention."

His rebuke may have been genuine but likely had come from a pang of guilt for having complained earlier.

"Too true," replied one of the men unknown to Kimon, sighing in heavy resignation.

"More like her *dishonor*," spat Tychon. A piece of unchewed meat flew from his mouth. "Her mother was a whore, sleeping with Zeus like she did, and that slut of a daughter left her husband too easily for my taste."

"But you have no taste," Kimon shot back. He knew Tychon always complained too much and couldn't hold his tongue, perhaps because its cage of teeth had so few bars, and they had so great distance between them, and those that remained were rusted from rot.

"Still," an older man growled, "he's got one point. After all, Paris tricked these Spartans by acting as if he were an ambassador on a diplomatic call to go and seduce her. How many of us would like such deception as a way to gain entry into a place where we didn't belong."

"And I heard she's already dead," said another soldier. "So why are we still fighting this war? Besides the fact that the Spartans are right outside, on the other side of these walls."

The one-eyed man stood again.

"I am Drakon," he announced. "Do not doubt that my ferocity does not measure up to my name!" Looking around him, he continued, "And I will flail anyone here who traduces our king or his choice of a queen."

"Relax, Drakon," interrupted Khristos, a local priest who had joined the battle out of his own sense of duty and as a comfort to his neighbors. "These men have been fighting for a decade now. They just want to know that there is an end in sight. That is not an unreasonable expectation."

"Thank you, Khristos," Kimon said. "Most of us here just want to get back to our wives and our lives. Ten years is a great toil when it is only our fight by accident of birth."

"Khristos," asked one. "Why would the gods allow this war to continue?"

"Perhaps Zeus wants to depopulate the Earth," the holy man answered. "It has been getting crowded as of late."

"I can move if Zeus wants," Tychon joked.

"And most of us will help you," Kimon jeered back to him. A fair number of those hearing this laughed and nodded in agreement. The tension having somewhat abated, the soldiers—or rather the citizens compelled into soldiery—settled in to pass another night of waiting, waiting for action. Or, better yet, a resolution to the last ten years—years of siege and repel, attack and counter-attack. Perhaps the only one looking forward to the morning was Drakon, who was indeed a professional soldier and aptly named.

The remaining "troops" settled into their customary patience that was not patience as much as time-killing anxiety. They killed time with routine before the war could kill them. Many moved among others to impart messages for their families should the worst happen.

Those lucky enough to have learned how to write wrote notes as well as their wills, then pocketed them in a *sáka*.

This pattern of customary boredom continued until several young men raised their heads, cocking them to one side.

"Hear that?" asked a boy, perhaps no older than fifteen. Others shook their heads in agreement while the older men looked on, puzzled for a moment until things became quiet enough and the sound loud enough for their ears. The noise of woodsmen—lumbermen, millers, and carpenters—rang in their ears. The clop of axes chopped through the air as trees were cut down. Then one could make out the grinding rasp of two-man saws slicing planks from the felled trunks. Finally, this ensemble was joined with a percussion of hammering as the wood was fabricated into—what?

The sounds continued for three days, yet no guard could report seeing any troop movement. The men passed puzzled looks to one another. While passing time playing rounds of dice, a random soldier might shout, "What are they doing?" Or, "Can you see anything yet?" up to the sentries, only to receive shrugged shoulders and a puzzled look as an answer. All the while, one question hung in the air.

What were those Spartans up to?

Men of Troy, Hoi Polloi 〜 Bill Cushing

The cacophonic chorus of woodworking kept on even as the sun set and groups of these men of Troy collected around small fires. Eventually, though, even the sounds beyond the walls faded, becoming background noise and just another part of the monotony as darkness enveloped these citizen soldiers.

By the third night, many retreated from the fires to line the thick fortress walls and sleep, although the best they could expect was a nap. Once all empty space had been taken, some simply lay on the ground using stones as a pillow or, if they had one, a helmet. Some even tried sitting back-to-back, using each other's weight as a resting place. Kimon noticed how bad that idea seemed as these men, eventually nodding off, fell to their sides, the fall jolting them awake.

At some point during the evening, slumber overtook the men not on guard duty as weariness conquered discomfort. Kimon himself finally drifted off as well.

"*Koita! Koita!* Look!"

Kimon was shaken awake and opened his eyes to see Khristos, who pointed to the makeshift turret closest to them. Kimon realized the shouting came from there. He watched an orange horizon spreading and draping the mountains beyond as the sun rose. Swiveling his head toward others calling similar proclamations, Kimon saw them pointing outside to the grounds, all aiming toward the same spot.

While they waited, Kimon and the other men still talked among themselves, speculating on what had happened outside the walls and why it was important enough to notify the general. They then noticed the general and his advisers leaving *en masse*, most likely to confer with others in command, perhaps even with the prince himself.

Helios made his way up the sky in his burning chariot toward the day's zenith. The men gossiped, speculated, and, of course, complained. What was happening? Where were the leaders? Why was no one telling them anything?

At last, a column of hoplites—regular army soldiers—marched toward the gates followed by a cordon of the highest-ranking generals, including Paris. Two of the soldiers lifted the iron beam barring the gates, no mean feat given that the locks had been in place so long they had become sealed with a coat of rust. Once freed of their near-decade-old shackles, the massive doors were opened, hinges creaking from the disuse of age.

Men jostled one another, jockeying for a good spot to view whatever it was that had captured such attention. As the portal opened, many gasped, exhaled, or whistled. Others, Kimon included, stood in numbed silence at what they saw. Standing at the entrance, Kimon saw the luckiest of good luck charms known to Troy: a horse, specifically a wooden steed standing more than forty cubits in height, pregnant with girth. It was mounted on a wheeled base that had been engraved with the words "To the glory of Athena."

Beyond that, the ground had been razed, and smoke rose from the remains of the makeshift barracks that had been built on the outer grounds during the third year of the war. Kimon tasted the acrid smell filling his nostrils. Remnants of burning embers still floated, like so many gnats, around those closest to the entrance. More than once, Kimon slapped away the stinging heat of those landing on his arms and shoulders.

Otherwise, there was no sign of the invaders anywhere. By all appearances, the armies outside the walls had given up—whether in surrender or frustration—and returned home. A group of five hoplites cut through the wooded area beyond the city's moat, taking the path toward the Aegean Sea to check for Spartans on the shoreline.

"Is it possible," one general said, "that we have won this easily?"

Upon hearing this, Kimon shook his head. Easily? He'd been at this place fighting for almost the entire life of his daughter. He hadn't seen his family in months even though they didn't live far from the encampment he'd been attached to. "Easily" was not a word that came to mind when he thought of what they had all been through.

But he wasn't about to let that get in the way now because it looked like all the battles, all the killing he'd seen and done, all the terror of constant war might be ending. He felt something he hadn't felt in far too many years—hope, even something that might be happiness, although it had been so long he couldn't be sure.

"Still," he thought—and then he heard shouting.

Men of Troy, Hoi Polloi ∽ Bill Cushing

"You!" yelled a captain, pointing at Kimon. "You there. Get over here. Help these men get this bounty inside."

Kimon trotted out the gates and joined five others straining on a lanyard. There were several other lengths of rope that groups were tugging as well, and with all their efforts, the crudely cut wheels at the statue's base began turning and the equine effigy began to move from outside through the gates. While the "volunteers" sweated and struggled to move the oversized figure, Kimon looked back over his shoulder to see the generals conferring with Paris.

Because the idol had been left by the Lion's Gate, it took hours of sweat-soaked effort to both remove the stones and loosen the stone pediment that, while protecting the city, interfered with clear passage of the statue. It was finally pulled far enough inside to close the gates.

By this time, the scouts sent out earlier had returned, reporting that even the coastline was deserted and emptied of any Spartan ships. The crowds of soldiers hearing this began believing that the gods had chosen sides, and the Trojans had been the favored *polis*.

Meanwhile the leaders still talked, occasionally breaking their formation to move around and investigate the effigy. Some pounded their fists on it. Others hammered their swords against its massive legs, its height being too great to go any farther up without a ladder or platform.

Finally, Paris signaled for them to join him in the nearest tent they could find—Kimon supposed, based on the last ten years of "hurry up and wait"—to discuss the current situation and reach a decision.

It was late in the afternoon when a captain, carrying several scrolls, marched out and called the men into line for an official announcement. He picked three men and, giving each a scroll, ordered them in several different directions to deliver parchments to the other defensive positions throughout the *polis*.

Having attended to the other sets of orders, the captain mounted the base of the wooden horse and ceremoniously unrolled the remaining parchment to address those before him.

"Men of Troy," he announced, projecting his voice to its fullest.

The barking command caused the sound of talking to go silent and the shifting, restless men to come to a standstill.

42

"Men of Troy!" he repeated, now with the tone of victory. "We have won the war against the Spartan incursion!"

"*Opa!*" many of the men shouted, their cries filling the area. "*Opa, opa!*"

Some thrust their makeshift spears, jabbing the air, while others, including Kimon, exhaled relief. War was done. They could go back to life. Kimon didn't pay much attention to what remained of the official orders; instead, he thought of a warm meal and comfortable bed for the first time in months and, more important, from now on. This damnable excuse of "a struggle for victory," as he had heard it put too many times in the past ten years, was done. Over. He was going home to his wife, his child, his family.

"For tonight," the captain's words brought Kimon back to the present, "this homage to Sparta's humility—our 'Trojan horse'—will rest here until we can find proper use for it."

With the troops formally dismissed, Kimon turned in his weapon and the pitiful excuse for armor, then trotted away from his station and turned toward his home. His step lightened in relief the nearer he got, and upon entering his home—a stone structure in bad need of repair after a decade of forced neglect, but there'd be time enough for that—he immediately swept his daughter in his arms, holding her tight while dancing in mad circles with the giggling girl.

"*Manoula, manoula!*" the child called out. "Come and see—*bampás* is home."

Seeing his wife run in from outside, Kimon lowered the girl and ran to his wife to kiss her, mostly with gratitude—any fervor having been drained from years on duty. They embraced as they hadn't in too long, leisurely and lingering as Kimon assured her that he was home for good. The war was done, and they'd now spend the rest of their lives together—in peace.

Pushing long black curls of hair from her face, his wife shooed Kimon to bed for a nap, promising him a grand welcome-home meal. He willingly obliged, for there would be time enough for passion later.

Hours later, his daughter entered the room to wake her father. Stretching his arms, an action he hadn't done in some time without risking hitting another man accidentally, Kimon got up. He shuffled out to the main room where his wife had spread a feast of sun-dried fish, bread, feta, nuts, and olives, along with something he had missed: a carafe of wine.

"Ah," Kimon intoned, clapping his hands together and rubbing them in delight, "what have we here?

"A feast for a king," and he winked to his little girl.

"No kings here, thank the gods," his wife replied as the three of them sat to imbibe. Laying her hand on his arm, she whispered, "Better than kings, I have my husband back."

Motioning "tonight, tonight" to her, Kimon settled down to the meal. He actually found it a bit challenging to relax and take his time eating; he'd become so used to wolfing whatever rations he had in anticipation of fighting that it had become habit. It was one he was happy to lose. After dinner, as they sat, sated, there was a knock at the door.

Khristos entered and gave greetings all around.

"I am just visiting those whom I know to see how they're doing," he told Kimon. "You and yours seem quite well."

Kimon nodded agreement, asking, "How does it go among the others?"

"As you can well imagine, everyone is very happy, what with our victory over the enemy," adding, "even though it makes little or no sense."

"I do not question good fortune, my friend."

"Ah, fortune," Khristos intoned. "Fortune is not a thing I care to rely on. It can turn about more quickly than a top. Did you hear about Cassandra?"

"What now?" Kimon asked. "What did she do now?"

"It was right after you left," Khristos sighed and grinned, continuing, "She came running to the gates toward the horse, waving her arms and shouting."

"What did she say?"

"Right after you left, she entered the area where the statue sits. She began screaming warnings. According to her, we are not to trust this 'gift' that we've received," and throwing his hands up in mock surrender, he added, "but you know her: always yelling about this and that, seeing bad fortune and disaster everywhere."

"True," Kimon agreed, "but she has been right in her predictions before. However, I am certain you are right. These are nothing more than the ravings of a woman seeing conspiracies and bad fortune everywhere. For myself, I am pleased to come home, lie in a real bed, and get some rest."

"Good for you," Khristos exclaimed as he stood. "Now let me go before I overstay any welcome I may have."

"You are always welcome here," Kimon told the holy man.

"Thank you, and thanks to your lovely wife and child," he said as he tousled the young girl's hair before leaving. "I hope to see you again soon"

"Me as well," Kimon hugged the man, "but for now, may we all rest in peace."

"That we shall," Khristos responded, giving Kimon an informal bow and salute. "Tonight we shall, all of us, indeed rest in peace."

∾

Named in honor of Civil War Naval Commander William Barker Cushing, Bill Cushing grew up in New York but lived in various states, the Virgin Islands, and Puerto Rico before moving to California, where he now resides with his wife and their son.

His short stories have appeared in the Altadena Literary Review, Borfski Press, *and the* Newtown Literary Journal. *"A Former Life", his poetry collection, was honored by the Kops-Featherling International Book Award.*

Bill earned an MFA in writing from Goddard College in Vermont and recently retired after twenty-three years of teaching at East Los Angeles and Mt. San Antonio colleges. He facilitates a writing group for 9 Bridges, a non-profit community of writers.

DYING INNOCENCE
RUBY G.

The graveyard was quiet, the night solemn. An eerie fog covered the ground. The moon's light shone through the clouds in thin beams illuminating a small number of gravestones located there.

Sam walked up to a newer gravestone—one only three years old. His son, Grant, was secured in the carrier on his back. His two young daughters, Elara and Emmi, walked beside him.

As they approached, the clouds slowly parted, and the moonlight shone directly on the gravestone, revealing the words etched on its marble surface.

Ebony Anne Shayde
March 9, 1983 - May 16, 2018
Army Veteran, Mother, Wife
May her name survive the test of time.

Sam stared at his wife's grave, a tight knot forming in his chest. It'd been three years since he'd seen her face, her beautiful brown eyes, her crooked smile. Three years since he'd felt her hand in his hair, her arms around his waist. Three years since he'd heard her heartbeat in his ear as he rested his head on her chest.

Three years since he'd become a single father of three...

And soon, unbearably soon, he'd become a single father of two.

Emmi ran up to the grave, her oxygen tank clanking as she dragged it behind her. She sat cross-legged in front of the marble tombstone with a smile.

"Hi, Mommy! We're back!" she said.

Sam watched as his youngest daughter talked excitedly to Ebony's grave. Telling it about her day at school, how her ballet lessons were going, and that she had her first dance recital coming up. She talked about how pretty she thought her dress was and how excited she was to wear it.

Sam's heart ached.

That recital was in eight months.

The doctors gave her six to live.

Emmi pulled out one of her favorite toys, a little stuffed bunny. She played with it as she leaned against the gravestone, a massive smile on her face.

Elara tightly grabbed her father's hand as she watched her naive little sister. The little sister couldn't comprehend that their mother wasn't there. The grave was just for show. All that was there was an empty decomposing shell of what used to be their mother six feet underground, but little Emmi didn't understand that. Little Emmi went on as if their mom was still there.

But their mom was gone.

And soon, Emmi would be, too.

Yet there she was, with an oxygen tank in hand, laughing and playing in a dark, eerie graveyard without a care in the world.

∾

Ruby G. Has been a storyteller nearly all of her life. She has long been aware that her passion and calling is to tell stories that will help and serve others, as well as to spread the truth and love of Christ wherever she goes. With a degree in English/ Communication and a minor in Graphic Design, she intends to create and speak through all forms of art and storytelling.

To read and purchase more of her works, visit www.rubygwrites.com

STORIES THAT MAKE YOU THINK

STARSHIPS & ROCKETS
THE POET Q

Visions of Starships and Rockets at an intergalactic traffic light. '70s Chevies outfitted for space flight—fuel stations on craters and vibrant neon lights. Today, we ride amongst shooting stars, replacing powerful engines and big rims with rockets equipped with extra propulsion and custom paint jobs that match the interior trim.

Let's glide from here to Andromeda, then to the Virgo Constellation for some fuel and a milkshake. There's a meetup in the Cigar Galaxy. It's the Ursa Major for all the space players in spacesuits that match all the way down to the boots and super fly ladies pulling up in their own space outfitted coupes.

Or we can just cruise around the Milky Way too. All I'm trying to say is wherever we go from here is up to you. I have additional fuel tanks and oxygen too. It doesn't really matter to me as long as I'm riding with you.

I awake from my dream, head cradled in the lap of my beautiful queen. Listening to motors burn through gasoline up and down the street in the summer heat. Bobby Womack is playing while enjoying the ocean breeze. Knowing that my love will always find you in this life and the next, you are my eternal peace.

∽

I'm an avid traveler and writer of my life experiences. Not everything I write is all sunshine and rainbows because life truly is a rollercoaster ride. I like to write about all the highs and lows and everything in between to let everyday people like

Starships & Rockets ∾ The Poet Q

you know that you are not alone and that you are loved. I hope you join me on my poetry exploits. You can follow my journey on IG: @thepoetq *and my blog* thepoetq.wordpress.com.

THIEF

KURT WAGNER

First and foremost, you should know that I am a thief, and it is the one thing I come by honestly.

Now, before you get that judgy look about you, pause here a moment and allow me to share my tale. I daresay you'll want to hear my every word.

I was born neither rich nor poor. My home was not broken, and there was no abuse I can think of that would have turned me down this path. There was no desire for anything tangible in my house, and I was cared for adequately enough not to need other people's things.

Friends came and went, same as with everyone, and companionship was available when I desired it.

No, no... don't get up. I'm only giving you my background to clarify that I am a thief by choice, not due to necessity or circumstance.

The first thing I remember stealing was twenty dollars from Nana's purse. I was three years old, remarkably astute for one so young, and had seen her open her bag at the store. I was sitting in the cart, so I'd had a great view. I remember it perfectly. A black-beaded coin purse with a matte silver latch that made a sharp "click" when it was opened. Inside were several soiled green bills folded several times over into a roll.

There was a smattering of coins, but I instinctively knew that those were small change, as it were, compared to the green roll inside. She pulled out the roll and unwadded it. She pulled out two old twenty-dollar bills from somewhere in the middle, but not before I saw that she had three left—along with two tens, a five, and seven ones.

53

We got back from the shopping trip, and Nana put her purse on the entryway table when she went to put her groceries away. An instinct stronger than any I'd felt before drew my hand to the zipper of her purse and slowly opened it without making a sound.

I tingled from head to toe with excitement as each zip opened, and I grew closer to my prize. My hand reached in as if a force directed it precisely to the black-beaded change bag, and my thumb and forefinger touched upon that silver clasp without even brushing another thing in that bag. I pulled quickly but gently, and it came away with a clink.

I froze. I'd forgotten about the coins, so focused was I on the greater treasure, a lesson, I assure you I never forgot.

My heart pulsed rapidly in my chest, and I was about to give up and put it back, pretending innocence, but that instinct kicked in again, and I took a breath.

My pulse slowed. I withdrew the coin purse and unlatched it smoothly, using my own spit as a lubricant to keep it from clicking.

I unfolded the roll of bills and grabbed a single twenty-dollar bill, quickly folding the rest of the wad back up the same as it had been and nestling the coin purse back in its proper position. The zipper was closed, and I was playing in my room by the time Nana came to check on me.

The thrills and excitement of that experience were more addictive than any drug.

You don't need to look so disbelievingly at me. I have no reason to make this up. At that point, I gained my initial awareness of how covetous I was and the sense of purpose that it provided.

From that day, I stole anything from anywhere. I raided pockets and purses that were left idle, as well as whatever was in the pockets or on the shoulders of people walking by.

I opened doors that were never meant to be opened by me, learning how to pick locks, overcome electronic sensors, and bypass biosecurity measures.

There was always an itch, though. Always something that tugged at my mind and told me it wasn't enough. That I wasn't good enough.

So, I pushed harder. I removed bags of treasure from armored security officers without them even knowing I had ever been there. The safety deposit boxes at banks were like taking candy from babies.

I was even so skilled in creating a program that could steal money while it was in transit between one computer to another.

There was nothing that someone had that I couldn't also possess.

Art from museums? Yes, please.

Weapons from dealers? If I desired.

There is no feeling more gratifying than knowing who you are and working every second to continue unlocking the potential contained within... or so I thought.

I can say, without ego, that I am the most talented thief I know of, and I know quite a few in the trade. There aren't conventions or meetings or anything like that, but still, like has a tendency to attract like, and I've met some of the best.

I've been offered countless jobs from countless shady individuals who didn't know my identity, only my skill.

I turned down all of those. I did what I did for me, not for anyone else, but, again, I must confess that sometimes the challenge was so intriguing that I would steal those requested items, just to see if I could, so that no one else could take them.

Hell, sometimes, I even put back what I stole before the person ever knew it was gone as a sort of "two-for-one" on the excitement.

I can tell you that I confounded quite a few people with my shenanigans. There were times I kept what I stole, but at some point, there really is such a thing as too much, and I wasn't much of a materialistic person anyway. I just liked taking what others thought was for them alone.

However, at some point, there comes a time in a woman's life when she has achieved the top in her field. Where her skill is so perfected that there really is no new challenge for her.

What is one to do when the purpose you've worked toward your whole life ceases to satisfy? This is a very disheartening time. If the thrill is gone, if there really is no more challenge, what then is the purpose?

Thief ∽ Kurt Wagner

I became desperate and looked for greater, even foolhardy, challenges. I have the US President's wristwatch and one of the Queen's earrings as evidence of that.

I had a moment when I thought using my skills for the benefit of others would give me the satisfaction I was desperately craving. I stole the funds from three of the biggest human trafficking rings in the world AND sent the authorities all of the files necessary to shut them down.

You know what happened? Nothing. Six new rings sprang up in their place, and things continued with barely a hitch. That wasn't the worst part. The worst part was that it did nothing for me. A few people saved, a few more lost. What did it matter?

I tried the same with some of the drug cartels—same result.

Hero-ing wasn't for me.

A therapist recommended travel as a chance to "reset" myself.

I'd already been to most places, and people, it seemed, were pretty much the same anywhere you went.

So, I was really at a crossroads in my life for the first time. I didn't know what was next for me. What does a master thief do when she has stolen everything?

I got my answer one evening as I stared distractedly into my fifth dirty martini at a dive bar in Singapore. An older couple next to me said something that caught my attention.

The topic, of course, was banal, but it was the way they spoke about their plans to travel that set a fire inside me.

I threw some money on the table, gave both of the men a giant kiss on the lips, paid for their meal, and virtually skipped out of the restaurant amid the gawks and stares of porters and patrons alike.

What was so inspiring? Oh, I want to tell you, but that would be too easy. Try guessing. I'll give you some hints.

Hint number one. It is something enormously precious.

No! Weren't you listening? Money became too easy.

Still no. Jewels or precious metals are so passé. Come on, try harder. I know you have more creativity than that.

Hint number two. It is so precious that it can't be quantified but so under-appreciated that it is often thrown out in a moment of emotion.

What? Do I mean water?

Time? Now, you're thinking more abstractly, but you're still wrong.

Last hint. When you don't have it, there isn't much reason for anything else. Not life either, though that is another fair guess.

What is it that put you on this plane today? Was it your job? Your family? We both know that your real motivation lies elsewhere.

What is that something?

Don't be afraid.

Go on, say it.

Yes! Hope. It is the hope that somehow, in some way, life gets better.

There are the surface hopes people cling to and believe are real when, in reality, they hold little weight. There are the hopes instilled by society. These, like the surface hopes, are believed to be significant, but they don't spark a person. Finally, we have the real hopes, the hopes that people don't even recognize they have. They are so deeply buried under false hopes that it takes some work to discover.

Oh, and when I do discover them... what a thrill. It is like owning a piece of a person. It is like having a secret that only I know. Possessing that secret requires that I learn all about you and get to know you better than you know yourself.

Let's take you, for example. You love your wife and kids. You work hard to succeed at your job, and you think you hope that life will reward you for your compliance.

I have news for you. Life doesn't do anything for you. You have to do it all for yourself.

The problem is that most people aren't aware enough to take that kind of action, to actively cast off their false notions and pursue that which will truly fill them with hope.

If you can't chase your dreams, what is your point in being? You're just going to be another person who wastes space. That is what I shall take from you. I take your complacency and strip you of your hopes for a false life.

Thief ∽ Kurt Wagner

While you've been sitting here, I injected you with a rare poison of which there is no known cure. It will begin eating away at your insides over the next several months. Each day will be increasingly more painful than the last. Your children, also, will not be coming home anymore. Remember those trafficking connections?

Your wife will, and I'm betting, be lost to a grief-driven suicide.

Don't look so surprised. I told you I was bored. A master without a challenge is… well, hopeless; and, as I can so clearly see on your face, you understand how absolutely awful hopelessness is.

The paralytic I added to the poison will wear off by tomorrow morning. The doctors will just likely think you had a minor stroke.

On some level, you should be honored. Do you know how much time I spent researching to choose you as my test subject?

I had to master a whole new skill set. Stealing items is easy. People are complicated. Picking a lock or hacking a computer is nothing compared to getting inside the human mind.

I'd say, "Good luck," but it would be insincere and pointless.

Oooo, I just had a thought.

What if, maybe, I'm lying?

Maybe both an antidote and your children can be discovered by someone who is gravely determined?

It would certainly be something to hope for.

∽

Kurt Wagner is a Kurt-of-all-trades who incorporates his many interests into his writing. He is a founding member of Morpheus Writers and has an MA degree in Education. He has been a high school and college English, mythology, public speaking, and creative writing teacher and professor for more than twenty years. He is also a certified instructor of SCUBA diving, first aid, wilderness survival, Parkour, gymnastics, and archery. Kurt has taken and taught many writing workshops. He has also taken part in Camp NaNoWriMo, James Patterson Master Class on Writing, and Algonkian. He has published a full-length novel entitled

The Vivid Dreamer, *completed a feature-length screen play, "Sage of Nexus Point," and published several short stories including "Cutter's Blood" (published in Hemingway Shorts). Kurt writes, designs, and creates a variety of games, award-winning poetry, original content for a variety of media.*

ENVY
REGAN W. H. MACAULAY

T he woman pauses and heaves a sigh. She clutches a live cricket between her index finger and her thumb. It wriggles for its life, which will end shortly. Not like her life. Not like theirs.

She is the woman at the end of the universe, and her time will never come. They are the creatures she looks after: the last of the Moca salamanders, the final pair of Bumble Frungit toads, a single Royal Fish of the New Siam government, and three mammals whose names are long forgotten. There are more—feeding them all is an endless and repetitive task. They are suspended in perpetual time. Immortal. Trapped. And they all eat crickets. That's all that's left to eat.

A Frungit toad laps the cricket from between her fingers. Squish. The toad gulps, swallowing hard. The cricket is gone. The woman's envy swells inside her like an angry flame.

∽

Regan W. H. Macaulay is an award-winning author of novels, short stories, children's literature, and scripts. Writing is her passion, but she's also a producer and director of theatre, film, and television. She is an animal enthusiast as well, which led her to become a certified canine and feline massage therapist. She is the author of The Trilogy of Horrifically Half-baked Ham, *which includes "Space Zombies!" (based on her film, "Space Zombies: 13 Months of Brain-Spinning Mayhem!" available on iTunes and DVD), "They Suck", and "Horror at Terror Creek". Coming soon, Regan's first middle-grade novel series,* Peter Little Wing.

ADMIT ONE
TYCHO DWELIS

WHACK! Schwwwwwwing. Ding! Thunk. His arm swung like a tree in a hurricane and smashed the hammer down onto the metal target, sending the ball up, up, up to kiss the bottom of the bell that sat at the top. It capped the fun-time obelisk that watched over the fairgrounds.

"Well, I'll be, sir," the metal-braced, sun-tanned, part-time teen muttered as he shielded his eyes from the blistering Dakota sun. "You're the first one to get it up there all day."

"Not the first time I've been first," the stranger replied, wiping a bead of sweat from his brow.

"You've won, uh, twenty tickets. You can exchange 'em over at the prize counter for somethin' nice, I'm sure."

The stranger took the yellow "Admit Ones" and stuffed them into a worn denim pocket. "Do you mind if I hang around here for a moment, swing a few more? You don't have to give me any more tickets. I just want to knock it around a little. Clear my head."

"No problem. Maybe you'll get some people to actually come over here. It's been dead all day."

Swing.

"So," the teen asked, "where're you from?"

Ding!

"Europe."

"Wow, really? That's a *long* ways away."

Swing.

61

Admit One   Tycho Dwelis

"Only a breath. Sailing's the easy part."

"What brought you *all* the way out here?"

Ding!

The stranger handed the worn rubber mallet back to Part-Time and clapped him hard on the shoulder. "Family."

The stranger moseyed his way through the rest of the Great Pumpkin Fall Festival, taking in the sights and smells. America was a strange place indeed. Crisp orange leaves fell to the ground like contented sighs and crunched beneath sneakers. A young girl threw her head into a trough filled with water and came up glistening, a ruby-red treasure between her teeth. Folks shooting air rifles at cans and tossing rings at rubber ducks lined the streets. Brown dead foliage baked in the afternoon heat, filling the air with notes of comforting decay. Something wafted in the stranger's direction… the smell of fresh pie.

The stranger found a single, hot tear forming in his right eye, and he quickly wiped it away with a large hand. Now was not the time for sorrow. Now was the time for deliberation. His brother was here. He knew it. He just did not know where. His brother's presence rumbled in his chest like distant thunder, but the location itself was indiscernible.

The stranger had spent three days looking around this small town of Highland (pop. 248). He had drifted about town, trying to follow an invisible thread to an invisible fly. That invisible thread had led him to a lovely fair at the edge of town, but not to his brother.

"Excuse me, sir! Would you like a slice of apple pie?"

The stranger turned to meet the eyes of a young woman, blossoming in the days of her glorious youth. In her hand, she gripped a slice of pie on a paper plate, and on her face radiated an unabating smile. She held a fork out to him and added, "It's free!"

The caramelized apples oozed from the sides of the crust and glistened in the afternoon sun.

The stranger smiled and took a piece. "Thank you," he said, "such generosity."

"We won the pie contest, so we made up a whole batch to hand out. Would you like whipped cream on yours, sir?"

25 Servings of SOOP

"Don't mind if I do."

The stranger leaned on the post of the tent and took the plastic fork from her. His eyes lit up when the crust hit his tongue, and he smiled at her in approval with the kindest blue eyes.

"This is rather good," he complimented.

"The secret's in the butter," she whispered, as though this great secret could shatter kingdoms. "So, what are you doing all the way out here, if you don't mind me asking?"

"I must stick out like a sore thumb."

"Pardon my forwardness," she apologized, "but when you live in such a small town, strangers tend to stand out."

"I'm visiting my brother."

"Sounds nice. He live around here?"

"No, he's just visiting. I was supposed to meet him, but I'm not sure where."

"Well, hopefully, he didn't go up to the caves thinkin' that they were gonna be open, 'cause they close down every year in August."

"I'll have to check there," the stranger added through a mouthful of pie. "Just up the road?"

"Yes, sir," she affirmed. "Up past the creek. It's a good hike, despite the caves bein' closed an' all."

"I really appreciate it, and thank you very much for the pie, Miss…"

"Liberty."

"It's good to meet you."

"You as well," Miss Liberty cooed as she leaned across the table. "What can I call you?"

"I prefer to keep my name to myself, Miss." Not today. Not the time.

"Got some dark history, Mister?" She toyed with the mystery just as she toyed with a dark ringlet of her hair.

"No. Just business, that's all."

Disappointment crossed her face, replacing her bright American-Apple-Pie smile.

The stranger stepped from the tent's shade back into the hot autumn sun and moved toward the dirt road that wound up the mountain. Flanked by tall,

63

bristly firs, the stranger felt right at home as he climbed through shaded patches of snow and cool air. The wind blew heavily through the trees for a moment, shaking them violently, and on the wind, the stranger swore he heard a voice.

Bring him home.

He climbed, following the signs that read: "Gift Shop" and "Cave Tours." A knot formed in his throat. The chill of the mountain's shadow pricked goosebumps on his forearms. What would he say? *Father's angry with you*, he supposed. *You've done a terrible thing.* Or maybe even, *how could you?*

The wounds still ran deep. They ran deeper than any root of any tree could ever run and deeper than any cave on the craggy surface of the earth. The stranger slipped on loose gravel as he trudged, and he spun the ring on his finger in his pocket. He had the habit of spinning the ring whenever his nerves rang high.

Normally, he was not one to get nervous. He throttled into everything with unmatched force and a full heart, nothing like what he felt now. Some part of him did not want to find his brother and hoped that the threat he felt tugging on his spine would lead him not to family but maybe to some great monster he was destined to slay instead.

His foot slipped on a patch of never-melting ice as he approached the door to the gift shop, which bore a sign that read, *"Closed for the season! See you next spring!"* He had not expected to find his brother there. His brother was better at hide and seek than that.

Left, his heartstrings told him, and he trudged farther up the mountain into the brush, past *"No Trespassing"* signs and mortal laws. The stranger feared what would happen when he *did* return home, with or without his brother, an empty seat at the table, regardless. And he feared the unbridled rage to come. He knew rage, but his father knew rage *better*.

The stranger finally found a cave where the web pulled strongest, a cold thing with a black entrance partially covered with brush, and he smelled fire. He pushed the brush aside and stepped through, crouched into the hole, his hulking frame a caricature in comparison.

When he came into the main body of the cave, the light of the fire danced across the walls, casting monstrous shapes in black and grey across crystals and sediment alike. A figure sat, planted on some dislodged boulder, and warmed himself by the fire. The stranger's feet crept across the earth, soundless, practiced, and the man at the fire did not notice until it was too late.

The stranger recoiled as the cave-dweller pulled a log from the fire, brandishing it like a club. After withdrawing, the cave-dweller flinched, adjusted his eyes to the darkness, and placed his hand over his heart in relief.

"Dear *God*, Thor, you can't just sneak *up* on somebody like that."

"I didn't want you to run."

Thor's brother swallowed, guilt in his eyes because he knew that was exactly what he would have done.

"We need to talk," Thor demanded.

Thor's brother sat back down on his boulder and returned the log to its rightful place in the fire. "About what?"

"You know *exactly* what. Father's in a fit, and Mother doesn't understand how to even *begin* to have a funeral. I-I…"

Thor clenched his hands into tight fists to tame his anger. His brother had done things before, terrible things, but nothing could compare to this.

"I'm sorry."

"Don't apologize to *me*. Apologize to Mother. Do you even mean it, Loki?"

Loki blinked into the fire and stopped prodding it. "No," he replied. "I don't think I do."

"Why would you do that? Baldr did *nothing* to you. He was always kind to you, Loki. We've always only been kind."

"Not Father," Loki spat. "Never, Father. I never asked to be judged by him, Thor."

"Father wants to protect you."

"I made things right the best way I could, the only way I knew how, and if Father compared me to Baldr one more time, I—"

"You'd kill him."

"What else was I supposed to do? Fair Baldr, Wise Baldr, Hero Prince, God of Truth. And I…?" Loki swallowed his words and gazed into Thor's eyes with eyes of his own, human eyes, boy's eyes. "So, what are you going to do?"

"I don't *know*."

"You're not going to drag me back to Father, are you?"

"I don't know!" Thor roared and slammed his fist into the cold rock wall that crumbled around stone-flesh, and the cave shook.

"Don't collapse my cave!" Loki hollered.

"I'm just stuck, brother," Thor huffed, an angry, sad, trapped huff, and he felt his eyes water. He strove to be tough, a battle-born warrior like his father, but the tears were too hard to stop. "He'll learn soon enough I found you. He knows everything."

Loki said nothing for a moment, and then, "Yes."

"His birds followed me. They followed me the whole way."

"I know."

"So, what do you want *me* to do?"

Loki drew his arm over his brother's shoulder, the comfort of a human body his only solace. "I'm not sure," he replied. "I'm sure there's no way out of it for me this time."

"I won't let Father do anything rash."

"He's going to kill me, Thor. An eye for an eye. That's how he is."

"I won't let him do it," Thor breathed through the tears. "If he kills you, I'll be all alone."

The brothers gazed into the fire, locked in an embrace and thought. The pondering did nothing, and the silence broke only after a log fell loudly into the fire.

"I didn't mean to kill him."

"Then *why* do it?"

Loki said nothing.

"Everyone loves—loved—Baldr. And Hödr? You *had* to go and rope him in? We haven't seen him for days. I fear he is dead."

"You don't understand, Thor. I hated him *so* much. Father throws away sons as one throws away scraps to dogs. What of Hildolf? Or Ali? Or Nep, or Vidarr, or any of the other brothers we never knew growing up because he kept them from us. I fuck a Frost Giant, and I am a traitor. *He* fucks a Frost Giant, and he is the *Father of Men*."

"You went and killed our brother, who was innocent in all this."

66

"He was not innocent. No son of Odin is innocent in this."

"So, you'd kill me then?"

"I almost wish Father had left me in the woods to die as an infant, and then I would not have known such suffering."

"I do not wish it," Thor replied.

Loki remained silent.

Thor clapped his brother on the shoulder, feeling no merriment leave his fingertips, and wiped his eyes. He said, "I'll leave you, brother, and attempt to give you as much time as I can. You may want to tie up any loose ends."

"Thank you."

Thor pulled Loki to his feet and locked him in an embrace worthy of two bears, cherishing their last moments.

"You are a good brother," he concluded.

Thor left the cave and began to make his way back down the chilled side of the mountain. Perhaps his father would be merciful. He ran his fingers over the yellow "Admit Ones" in his pocket and gazed up at the sky, where two ravens flew, intertwined, to report back to their master.

∽

I'm Tycho— I love storytelling and am incredibly passionate about writing, art, and anything that allows me to create my own worlds. My goal is to write dreamy fiction that is unique, inspiring, and imaginative. I like to write about numerous themes, some of which include coming of age, mythology and folklore, identity, relationships, and bullying. My books are intended for readers ages eight to twenty-five, and are meant to connect the world of the fantastical to everyday life.

I currently live in Colorado and just earned my MA in Publishing!

ROUND MIDNIGHT
CELINE ELIZABETH

The new moon stood before the grand sun, much like a fan stands before his favorite celebrity. He often amassed these moments in his heart since he only had a few minutes in passing. He was blinded by her beauty like most celestial bodies that were drawn to her gravitational powers. The lover he could never have. He could feel the power of her gaze etch itself into his rough skin. At this moment, his world was before him, her voice a gentle cosmic wind, her longing as strong as a cosmic storm.

The sun felt alone in this galaxy, despite the love of her orbiting subordinates. Mercury and Venus had stayed the same for centuries. Reserved. They didn't stimulate her mind. For the one who had the center of attention, she felt far from it. As though she were invisible. Even the sun has dark days. Then she looked at the moon before her. He was something different. She found herself drawn to him, and, as though the galactic tables had turned, she was caught into his pull.

"I am so happy to see you again!" Her voice was genuine, flavored with intrigue.

"I looked forward to meeting my Queen," said the moon as her rays brushed his face with an uncertain kiss. "What is it?" he asked.

"I am troubled," she said without hesitation, knowing their time was short. "I rule this system, yet I know little of its affairs." She paused for a second and lit up excitedly as she made her sudden request, "Won't you tell me of Earth? It must be exciting with those humans!"

The moon hesitated, "I... have little to say."

He didn't want to disappoint her with the things he had seen. The night brings with it terror and conflict, two things the sun has never known. Things that she should not be bothered with.

"There must be many stories to tell! Humans are God's most special creation!"

He had never seen her so excited. "That may be… but my light shines down on the worst of the race. The worst things are done in the dark. My light doesn't convict them. It feeds them."

"No, there must be some good thing there!" she pleaded. "Surely, there's something you've missed."

The moon shifted to the side slowly, and her face became distant. He wanted to please her. He wanted to be the one that relieved her from her disconcerted heart. "Make your request, and I'll strive to do it," he stated.

She raised her voice so that her wish would not be swept away by the wandering specks of dust of deceased universes. "Next time we meet, tell me at least one good story of the humans."

His soul grieved at her wish. He questioned if they had any good in them at all, but he accepted nevertheless. He had been the guardian of the Earth for as long as he could remember. He had seen floods and fiery destruction, countless wars and suffering, the murders of the night, and the corruption of humans. "If God Himself didn't create me, I wouldn't have believed He existed from seeing this Earth." He whispered to himself.

The moon looked back at the Earth, which was cluttered by the many lights of civilizations. He watched closely, beyond the blood-soaked lands, riddled by humans whose next heartbeat was fueled by war. Clouds rolled before him, blocking the slaughter. "The rain falls on the blessed and the damned, but my moonlight always catches the damned. Perhaps I am cursed."

"You… cursed?" the Earth moaned softly. "You are not qualified to say that. I am a victim of their force, yet you groan as though it's your body they carve into or your hair they shave."

"Then you understand my disposition."

"I cannot because even I know you cannot call a handcrafted creation damned. There is good." The clouds parted as the Earth continued. "Consider this man and his family." The moon shone his light on a makeshift raft with a dark blue sail. On it was a man, his pregnant wife, and a young boy. The sea was vast, with no islands in sight for many nautical miles. The waters a deep abyss with only his reflection looking back at him.

"What of them?" the moon asked.

"They are fleeing from the war. The father is a government official who is on the rebels' most-wanted list."

"Are they suffering from the man's sins?" the moon questioned.

"Pure of heart," the Earth replied. "I overheard your conversation with the Queen. You should observe them."

The moon interrupted, "To convey their deaths?"

"To learn of goodness and love since you are ignorant of those definitions." The moon fell silent at the Earth's comment. Even though they were friends, there are things a friend has to discover on his own. Sometimes all you can do for a friend is be a compass. You can guide them along a path, but they must decide whether they turn back or traverse further.

It was about midnight. The wife slept at her husband's side, and their young son slept at hers. They had a bed sheet spread over them, some pieces of wood, and a duffle bag with supplies that he had not yet seen them reveal. The wind was cold, and the waves were calm.

The man stirred, opening his eyes. He began to weep. Silently. Brokenly. He took a bitter breath and watched the moon against the black veil of space. "God, thank you for the moonlight." The man whispered, wiping his tears with his free hand as he cradled his wife in the other. The moon felt something in his core when he heard it.

"Perhaps I shall observe them," he said to himself.

On the second night, he found them floating once more on the Mediterranean Sea. They had fashioned a shelter with four posts and a tarpaulin roof. The father was looking up at the stars, lost in contemplation. The boy emerged from under the tarp, "Mother is asleep."

His father nodded before inquiring, "Why aren't you sleeping?"

"Who can sleep on a wooden raft that's floating into the void?" the son replied.

The father adjusted the small sail. "I'm steering us to better."

"Is traversing the untrained sea to seek refuge in an uncertain land really better?"

The father sighed, "I'm doing the best I can."

"If you were doing your best, then why are we here?" his son asked resentfully. The father didn't respond. "Is it true you did what those men accused you of?" his son questioned.

"No."

"She died because of you…"

They both grew silent as their eyes caught onto the fog that was rolling in. It looked eerie in the moonlight. The waters were uneasily still. He spun around, but visibility became poor. It felt like a nagging presage to the man. They couldn't trust themselves to know where the flooring was. They stood still in silence until the round moon hovered over them once more. His son then retreated under the tarp.

"Lord, let death not be our fate. My family has much to live for. I have lived my life, serving as honestly as I can. If I die, then I die, but my family… let them live."

The moon repeated the words to the sun.

"What do you think?" she asked.

"I think the prayer was selfish. He would accept death and let his family suffer without him."

"I think he's selfless. He wants his family to live because he hopes life will treat them kindly in his absence."

They were nearly out of supplies. Rain had not fallen for them to replenish their canteens. "You're doing your best," His wife reassured him.

"We should meet land soon. Hopefully, we don't have any more shark encounters," he said, placing one hand on her stomach.

"It was a small shark."

"It was still a shark," he replied.

She kissed him on his cheek. "How are you holding up with Marc?"

"He blames me for Marisol's death, but I can't deny it. I couldn't protect her."

"You tried all you could. We barely got out!"

Round Midnight ～ Celine Elizabeth

"They slaughtered her because I sought justice. She died because of me, Linda."

"Daniel…"

"He's right, but I can't lose you all. I won't," he replied.

"We will all make it," Linda assured him, smiling at her stomach.

With only the moonlight to guide them, they could see a faint structure that appeared to be sinking. "Is that… a boat?" Marc asked, pointing into the distance. He looked out at a form that grew larger and larger, materializing into a ship. At first, he thought it had no sail but soon realized that it had blended into the night because it was black. *Pirates.*

They retreated into the shelter, praying that they hadn't been sold out by the light of the moon. The raft peeled the seas apart as it advanced. The moon saw the quality of humans on the black sail ship. They were cursing and hollering at one another, with guns in their hands and loot at their feet. They were busy terrorizing the unfortunate soul that they had found adrift at sea.

The moon grew concerned. "Earth, lend me use your clouds to cover my light."

"I cannot summon clouds," stated Earth.

"The pirates will see them."

"And?"

"His wife is with child!" the moon pleaded. Thick clouds slowly rolled over the sea, blocking the moon's line of sight. "I thought you couldn't call them?" the moon inquired.

"They were already rolling in. You were too concerned to notice," Earth replied. The moon felt relieved.

The next night, Daniel told Linda that there was a storm brewing and warned her to stay under the shelter. He begged her, saying he couldn't lose her, confessing his love for her and the family, reiterating that he would not lose them like he lost Marisol. All the while, the round moon looked down on him, standing alone, talking to empty space on the raft. The midnight before, his wife had stepped into the ocean, thinking they had come ashore. His son jumped into the water after her but struggled to swim. Daniel was again forced to make a difficult choice.

25 Servings of SOOP

"He saved the one who hated him most!" the moon exclaimed to the sun.

"A mother will give her own life for her child to live."

"But she was with child!" the moon refuted.

"Her choice wasn't selfish," the sun replied.

They could see lights littering the coast as the stars did in the night sky. Dehydrated, disoriented, and seasick, Marc murmured, "You didn't have to save me. I really hated you."

Daniel weakly responded, "I love you even though… you hate me." There was only the howling of the night's cold uncomforting winds. They wondered if the coast was real, but all they had was hope and faith that God would blow their sail to it. The moon knew they would reach it, but Daniel was treading lines of consciousness as thin as the shadow of a hair.

An empty turtle shell was his pillow for the night but could have also easily functioned as his tombstone. "Father… stay with me," Marc pleaded. "No… I'm sorry… stay! Please…" The moon beamed his light down brightly on them.

It was around midnight when they were found on the coast. They were rushed to emergency care.

For a while, the moon did not see them until one night when Daniel came out of the hospital building. Daniel looked up to the sky and took a deep breath. "Lord, I thank you for life. My son's life and my own. I thank you for my wife and my daughter. For lending me their presence. Thank you for protection from the seen and unseen. For the sea and the creatures that fed us, and, Lord… I thank you for the moon that lent us its light."

"Now, you both know that you aren't cursed," whispered the sun.

∾

Celine Elizabeth, born on October 1, 1995, in the small Caribbean Island of Trinidad, is a newly published author with a passion for the English Language and the God who crafted it. Though writing is her primary passion, Celine often works alongside young people as a mentor and a tutor. It is her heart for Christ combined with her desire for educating and molding young people, that moved her to write her first book, Things That They Don't Tell New Christians. *She hopes to soon expand her portfolio and present more of her writings to the world. She draws inspiration from authors C.S. Lewis and Alexandre Dumas.*

THREE FRIENDS

E. A. ROHRMOSER

They were inseparable, the sharp-looking deep thinker dressed in cynicism, the insecure writer with the savior complex, and the fiery sculptor seeking to reshape her past. Three young spirits found each other at the base of a mountain, eager to climb, their paths pointing upwards. They stepped out from their myths to seek knowledge in the Tree, looking to disrupt the stable grounds of their preferred fields. All three were impressive in their potential, having each taken their first steps toward their revolutions, each unwilling to bare their self-doubts naked in front of the others.

Samael fashioned himself the leader of the threesome, always knowing what to do and where to go next. His disbelief in standard values made him appear fearless and self-serving. He looked like he came from wealth. Never having spent a night of hunger or cold, he still grew up to rebel against the hands that fed him while he wore the clothes they made for him. His chosen antagonists kept him warm while he declared a philosophical war on reality, blasting several essays through which he questioned the moral fabrics of existence. He always smiled and always knew exactly what was going on. A walking contradiction, it was as easy to love him for his confidence as it was to hate him for his selfishness. His determination made the others regularly trust his decisions, even though he led them through wrong paths on more than one occasion.

Adam was the other side of Sam's coin. He was a relatively quiet and vacant self-doubter who mostly enjoyed spending time by himself, always carrying the burden of worry for what he saw as wrong in others. In contrast to Sam's spontaneous banters peppered with vulgarity, he was brief and respectful in his words. His difficulty managing emotions was reflected in regular bouts of frustration when things didn't turn out as planned. His insecurity probably came from a bullied childhood. He dreamed of changing his world into a better place, choosing to do so through writing stories about love, family, and faith. Although the first of his books had been successfully published recently, he was still insecure about its relevance.

Lilith was the balance between the two men. A tomboyish majesty who thought she always knew exactly what she wanted. She enjoyed letting herself be driven to the unexpected whenever she felt she had decided to do so. Moody and explosive, her sharp humor turned into sharp statements whenever she sensed she was being attacked, a frequent occurrence. Decisive, she would simply storm out of a room if she didn't feel in control of the situation. She didn't care about words or ideas. She shaped her thoughts through sculpting, an art form in which she had innovated by incorporating non-traditional tools and materials to create new beauty standards. She gave almost no hints about her past, but a hint of damage from loved ones was implied in her character.

After proving their worth and taking residence in the Tree, they met each other while perfecting their crafts. The three of them connected under the common banner of unconformity, and they found a sounding board in one another. They would spend hours critiquing each other's ideas, with their disagreements diverging toward angry discussions, usually with Sam and Lilith vociferously bashing each other. At the same time, Adam wrapped himself in a cloak of his silence. Sometimes Lilith would turn her anger toward Adam for not supporting her point of view, which would pressure him into defending her against Sam. Sam's self-assured smile would never fade, not even when the other two conspired against him. He enjoyed them very much, and their incessant challenges made him feel important. Adam had rarely found others who could hold up a conversation through his young life and share his dark sense of humor as Sam and Lilith did. Lilith had found a voice for her thoughts in Sam and ears for her words in Adam, her gallant companions she could never break, no matter how sharply she chiseled them. They would spend hours unwinding from their great debates, intoxicated, sharing war stories about past exploits, with the narrative usually gravitating toward their sexual conquests. Sam would paint himself the philanderer, telling unbelievable, but very detailed, accounts of him spending many nights with many lovers.

Adam seldom spoke of a couple of brief and meaningless encounters, instead showing more interest in Sam's nuanced depictions. Sam usually pressured Lilith into sharing stories about her past romances. She never gave away names or details, but one time she shamefully confessed that it was only one past lover who had been able to make her reach climax. Sam always wanted to know more about Lilith's lovers—who they were, how many were there. Those impertinent questions would always be followed by Lilith's anger toward Sam, and Adam jumping to her defense. Lilith would regularly fall asleep on Adam's safe lap in the aftermath of those word battles while Sam would take off by himself, searching for further adventures.

They enjoyed visiting the outside world together with all its characters and scenarios, serving as an inspiration for their work. On this particular hot summer afternoon, sitting on a midtown bench, Sam ranted about the lives of others. He observed how their clockwork routines turned men and women into mindless animals, going back and forth with no ultimate purpose, just cogs in a useless machine. Adam expressed his partial agreement, countering with his belief that there was an actual purpose to this repetitive pattern, but just not the right one, as these men and women followed the wrong paths. Lilith laughed at them, mocking their inability to enjoy a moment of peace and quiet. Sam asked her to break the tie. Did she think the story went on with no purpose at its end or did it all serve an end purpose? Neither and both was her answer, telling them that the story goes on with no end but that the purpose was the story itself. She believed that the present was the only moment worth caring for, although with an eye slightly open to the next day. Both men were appeased with her balanced, and perhaps very polite, effort to hush them. After reaching harmony, Lilith sat quietly with a vague expression, looking at these clockwork midtown men and women. The afternoon sun reflected in her eyes, giving the impression that they shimmered on their own. Neither of her two companions dared to break the moment, and both wondered if anything about that scene had triggered a past emotion in her.

Eventually, they made their way away from the crowds, reaching an isolated field split by the path they were walking. The air was warm, and a mild breeze caressed their faces. As the sun settled, it gave the world a golden hue. All three were silent and a little nostalgic. Their aimless stroll led them to an abandoned property, a small housing structure marginally consumed by the nature around it. It stood in a wide pasture of yellow-green grass, a short distance away from the main path. An old crooked acacia stood to its right, its crown hunching toward the house, giving the impression that together they formed a virtual archway leading further into the grounds.

Toward the horizon, a pond with waters swaying with the summer breeze bore small waves with golden crests of the sun's reflection.

The threesome entered the structure to find a deserted small home, far from indulgent. Although there was nothing outstanding about the place, Sam, Adam, and Lilith took their time to explore the house and its remains. There was a story here to be read from three different vantage points. The old rotten furniture gave signs of a family of four having been its former occupants, most likely two parents of small children. They had to live uncomfortably, given the size of the structure; however, they made an effort to turn the place pleasant with meek ornaments. Lilith cleared the grime from one of its few windows to discover a view of the pond in the back, making her hands dirty in the process. Adam found an old trunk below one of the beds and opened it to reveal several treasures of stone and twig, put together by the parents to serve as toys and trinkets for their children. Sam reached inside to grab a river rock with a smiling face drawn in it, attached to a bundle of hay made to look like a stick figure with arms and legs. Sam turned slowly while staring at the drawn face, walking away with short steps. His usual forged smile was absent, and Adam caught a glimpse of a tear exiting his right eye before he turned his back to him. Lilith turned from the window to notice Sam's melancholy and stared at him quietly without him noticing. Adam proceeded to close the trunk and push it back below the bed, standing up to see Lilith exiting the house. Sam's haze was interrupted by Adam signaling him to follow him and Lilith outside the house.

They stood below the virtual archway of tree and house to admire the pink sky of twilight surrounding the sun as it set behind the shiny pond. In silence, each traveled back to a different past and the different paths that led them to this enchanting moment together. Lilith smiled and broke the silence with a chuckle. She took a couple of steps in front of Sam and Adam and turned to look at them smiling. She proceeded to remove her clothes, exposing her sprinkled naked body to the summer warmth and her companions' gaze. She then turned around, running and laughing toward the pond, jumping in with a loud splash. Sam and Adam looked at each other and broke into laughter. Hurriedly, they both removed their clothes to follow Lilith into the water. They splashed and laughed like little children whose most treasured possession was the joy of being surrounded by magic.

By nighttime, they lay by the shore on their backs, staring at the stars. They quietly traced the shiny dots with their fingers to draw invisible lines. Nobody said a word, and nobody dared ruin the wistful moment. Hours later, Lilith stood up to collect her clothes, which had been spread in all directions by the imprudent wind. She dressed and sat down near the main path to wait for Samael and Adam. Both men eventually caught up to her, ready to return to the Tree. Adam offered his hand to pull Lilith up, and the three of them walked back to their shared home, with the moon lighting their path and each's own fate and knowledge imminently driving them apart.

∾

E. A. Rohrmoser is a self-published author of literary fiction—raised by books, music, TV, and film—currently working on a collection of five stories that explore human talent and the struggle to break outside of traditional beliefs.

BEND AND BREAK
MARY RAMSEY

The Latina warrior arched her back, letting the moonlight bathe her in its beauty. *"Nice view for a literal garbage dump."* That's me, Sundra Cortez, code name: Sunshine. I was a runner from the wrong side of the streets. A dark Afro-Latina girl, rocking her natural curls.

And that sexy white boy, holding me close in his Italian-Croatian arms; my partner in crime, my ride-or-die: Antonio Varga, or "Deadlock."

"You're thinking about something, aren't you, Sunny?" The silver spoon vigilante was the son of a billionaire daddy and a third-wife mama. Although Mama was the one who taught him how to fire a gun and eventually make a side hustle out of building custom models.

I gripped his back hard, pressing my lips to his ear. "I'm thinking about how a nice boy like you ever got stuck with a name like Deadlock."

"Funny, Sunshine."

"Wasn't meant to be." I bit his earlobe, just hard enough to give it a tug. It had been a long week of hand delivering documents, dead bodies, all while running from the cops. Did I mention my forty pounds of armor that allows me to deploy my gravity skates? *A great core workout but not nearly as fun as it sounds.*

Whatever the heck Tony wore to work, it sure as hell wasn't armor. I could play connect the dots with all the bullet wounds. Still, none of that mattered once the gear came off. "Ow, do you really have to poke me in the ribs?"

I was lost in the loving gaze of his mocha brown eyes. When we heard a thunder crash, followed by the sound of fire.

25 Servings of SOOP

"What the fuck?" Tony grabbed his vinyl uniform pants, which still held his tool belt.

I took a moment to make myself decent, even if that meant putting on Tony's shirt and boxers. I also made sure to reach for my service weapon. There was usually no one around the junkyard this late at night, especially this far out into the desert of the free nation of Arizona.

It was clear what had made the noise. "Is that a body?" There was a human figure lying in the lone road. Yes, in it. The figure was resting, unmoving, inside a shallow crater surrounded by blue flames.

"This doesn't seem like actual fire," I said out loud to myself. Kneeling down, I could reach the human's hand. I gave it a hard tug, moving his limp arm outside of the ring of light. "Ouch! Nope, that's actual fire." Despite the heat of the flame, the man was freezing. His clothing seemed to be made of metal and plant fibers. And his body seemed to be immune to any physical pain.

"I think he's still alive," Tony said from the opposite side of the body. "I can see his chest moving."

Given Tony's expertise, I trusted his judgment. "We need to get him inside." I glanced around, looking for a way to free the body from the blue flames.

"Grab the tarp," Tony shouted, pulling me back.

I did as he asked, running for a vinyl tarp that we sometimes used to keep out the rain. Tony immediately grabbed it from me and threw it over the body and the flames. When he managed to get the figure wrapped like a fish in a net, he dragged the body closer to our hideout's entrance. That was when I got a good look at the man's face.

He was Caucasian, maybe in his early fifties, with grayish-blonde hair. As tony helped him onto our bed, the man's eyes opened, revealing metallic blue retinas. "What year is this?"

"2049," I said cautiously. "Are you injured?"

He swallowed hard, struggling for breath. "I don't know."

"What's your name?"

"I am called Abaddon." He moved his arm, repositioning himself to sit up. "What is this place?"

Tony was at our makeshift kitchen, heating a coffee pot. "Welcome to New Phoenix, a property of independent Arizona. You a time traveler or something?"

"Is time travel a technology you know of in this era?"

"Either that or you're an escaped convict from the banished lands," Tony said as he reached for a food packet. "All weary travelers are welcome here." He mixed the dry powder into the water to create an electrically charged tea.

"What is this?"

"Just a life-ration. Here in our time, they're easier to come by than solid food. Some places even use them for payment."

"I am grateful for your kindness and hospitality."

"Hospitality," Tony chuckled. "I haven't heard that word since I was knee-high to a grasshopper."

I was about to comment about Tony's old-school southern charm when I saw Tony's phone go off. Instead of ringing, it vibrated with flashes of red and blue. Deadlock had a job to do.

I reached for the phone as Tony got dressed. "Who do you think it is?"

"The caller or the target?" Tony asked.

"It's always the same caller," I sighed as I tossed him the phone before turning my attention to Abaddon. "Tony works for the government in a freelance capacity."

"Understood," Abaddon said as he took a sip of the nutritional broth.

"The target is a Taiwanese male, foreign national smuggling in non-GMO seeds. And not our houseguest." Tony gave a nod in my direction. "Abaddon, you're safe to stay here as long as Sunshine allows. If you try anything, she can cut you down with her bare hands."

"I can also protect you, the way I've always protected Tony and our beautiful home." I stood up to give Tony a kiss goodbye.

"I know you love me, Sunny." He left on his motorcycle, driving off into the desert, under the smog-filled sky.

I smiled, overwhelmed with love for my bad-ass superhero boyfriend. Leaning against the make-shift building as the cool desert breeze caressed my thighs. I slipped my hand into Tony's boxers, tracing my hip muscle between my legs. I closed my eyes, dreaming of Deadlock's stealth, the way he could cut someone's head off before they even knew he was in the room. I'd only seen it happen a few times when we were on conjoined missions. The idea of someone strong, who could protect me, kill for me, maybe even die for me, was a high unlike any other.

Suddenly, I felt another hand upon my thigh, a rough, masculine hand, touching me in a way that sent shivers down my spine. "Is that you, Abaddon?"

I could feel his facial hair, rough against my cheek. "If you want me to stop…"

"No." My thighs were trembling, and my heart felt weak as a jolt of pure, intense pleasure emanated through my hips. I arched my back, leaning into his touch, as he guided me to the bed. He continued to place pressure on my body, rubbing my skin with low, tender vibrations.

"Vibrations?" I placed my hand upon his, guiding him away (for the moment). I turned to face him, kissing his lips soft and slow. I reached between his legs, hoping to repay Abaddon for his generosity. But much to my surprise and embarrassment, all I could feel were scars.

Before I could ask any questions, his eyes met mine. "Where I'm from, our bodies are modified at birth so that we will never crave what we never know.

"What other parts are you missing?" I asked, my cheeks already flush with awkward discomfort.

"I am primarily an enhanced being, evolved for combat and stamina."

"Are you human?"

"No."

Somehow that answer made me curious, even flirty. "You feel human." I walked my fingers down his chest. "What does the world look like where you're from?"

"I come from a difficult time where love and compassion are relics of a past long forgotten. And all we have left is to await the great equalizer."

"Death." I cupped my hand to his face. Whatever he was, he could feel, and his body reacted to Tony's life-ration. Although his mind remained calm, his life force rippled with energy. "Is that why you came here? To know love?"

"In a manner of speaking."

I moved closer, pressing my forehead to his as if trying to truly understand. "From what year have you traveled?" Before he could answer, I kissed his lips.

His mouth tasted dry and cold. "2181. It is known in our history that in the timeline, there will be a man who will set into motion a series of events leading to the creation of my kind."

"You want to destroy your existence?"

"I do not want to die. Especially after what I just experienced at the hands of your beautiful form. But my world should never come to pass."

I was drawn in. This was the adventure I wanted, the life I wanted. "Do you need help?"

"You would aid me in my quest?"

"Tony and I, we have some valuable skills. It's been a while since we had a real reason to use them."

Abaddon sighed, a voice of reluctance. "Ah, yes, Tony."

"It's not Tony, right? That's not who you're here to eliminate," I said with a forced chuckle.

"Sometimes one's heart can be in the right place but still result in opening the mouth of hell."

The idea had my mind and heart twisted into a painful knot. I took his hand, stroking his fingers. That was when I saw it: the words "ride or die" on his inner wrist. Maybe he had the words from a long time ago. Maybe they represented someone else entirely. But something about him just felt right. "Let's roll."

∽

Mary Ramsey was born in San Francisco, but is a woman of the world. She joined the Air Force after finishing school and earned a bachelor's degree in cinema from San Francisco State University. Bouncing around from base to base opened her eyes to the greater world surrounding her and awakened her latent creative side. Mary combines her love for unique superheroes based on underrepresented minorities and the LGBTQ community with her desire to craft her own blend of romance, horror, and fantasy novels.

HIS DIVINE BALCONY
MADHUSHRI MUDKE

On most winter mornings, he would pull himself out of his bed with great enthusiasm to watch birds from his balcony. He would sit for two hours in his reclining chair with coffee in one hand and the newspaper in the other. Finally, at around quarter to ten, he would find himself in the kitchen making breakfast. He would present this breakfast to his wife in bed, and she would wake up with a smile. It is a sunny winter morning in the town of Maragoan. The town is known in India for its greenery and its cleanliness. Its citizens particularly appreciate it for the birds and wildlife that thrive within dense green, shrub forests, and cleverly manipulated gardens. The town has a tropical, dry savanna-like climate—temperatures range from forty-five degrees Celsius in summer to as low as ten degrees Celsius in winter.

It is a regular morning for Nahor. The birds are chirping, and there are three sparrows fetching grains from the sparrow box that hangs in his garden. Today, he feels an unusual warmth in the wind, something he hadn't felt in a while since the temperatures had dropped by almost ten degrees, reminding him of the start of winter. He was probably excited about Sahana's visit. It had been ten years since he met her at an outdoor event called Nature1990. This annual event was organized by an informal group led by affluent businessmen and doctors in the town. The event had experts who taught local residents about spiders, bees, birds, trees, and grasses.

On the cold Sunday morning of December 23, 1990, Nahor and Sahana were leading the group as experts in their respective fields. When he met her for the first time, he felt a tickle in his stomach. When he was alone, he felt her aura all around him. As soon as he found himself dreaming about her, he was pulled back to reality by a pair of golden orioles that called out loudly—an adult male and a female sat atop a flowering raintree right outside his home. He watched the pair forage for food and took the first sip of his black coffee. The sun shone golden rays upon the raintree. The yellow orioles looked brighter than the sun. He watched them with a smile.

Sahana was a professional dendrologist. She grew up in an all-girls' school and was extremely notorious. She used to beat up other girls in school and was tagged as a "mad-woman" by her teachers and fellow students. They all laughed at her and made fun of her. She was a living joke. It bothered her a lot, but she had learned to live with it.

Her mother was an extraordinary lady. Her mother portrayed emotions through art—oil on canvas! Sahana gazed at the paintings for hours whenever she stumbled upon them. She had framed her mother's paintings and hung them on the walls in their enchanting, little home. Sahana's favorite painting had a blue color palette with a mother and daughter watching stars in the night sky. She framed this one in a deep red, handmade paper and hung it above her study table. She never got bored of looking at this particular painting. She woke up staring at it and slept only after a quick glance. The painting was so pleasing to her that it never failed to put a smile on her face. For her, the painting resembled a complex relationship between nature, the mother, and the child. In her young mind, she could never understand why she loved these elements of nature and the relationship between a mother and a child more than anything else.

Even today, while she worked as a professor in the State University of Iowa, the painting hung in her study as a reminder of all her beautiful memories at home.

Nahor and Sahana were both barely twenty-five when they met at Nature1990. They had both just graduated and were well known within their nature-enthusiast community. They made a great team, and everyone loved their educational sessions on birds and trees. Sahana was a fun educator who often loved cracking inappropriate, dark jokes in her sessions. No one but Nahor would find her jokes, wrapped in satire and honesty, amusing. She would look at him and smile in between sessions just to be reassured that her thoughtful joke made her buddy chuckle. Nahor on the other hand was a no-joke man. He took his sessions rather seriously. He gave heavy assignments and made people take short quizzes during his educational sessions on birds. Sahana knew all the answers and she often announced them loudly to distract the whole session. The children in the group laughed at her and never took Nahor's classes seriously. Nahor hated it, but still, he never complained. After every outdoor session in the park, they would wave goodbye to the group and walk back from the venue to Nahor's home.

Nahor would make tea for Sahana, and they would drink it together. Nahor hated tea, but it was Sahana's favorite drink. They would engage in short, intense conversations about life and relationships, sitting on the floor of his balcony while slowly sipping tea. The conversations would quickly escalate to holding hands, short pecks on the cheeks, and fierce eye-to-eye stares. Eventually, they would both end up in his room, naked on the bed, under his warm blanket. He could never stop kissing Sahana until she slapped him hard to let her go.

They met frequently, explored the town, and made love endlessly. They both knew that this relationship of theirs had no name nor any legal strings attached to it. It was purely a lustful endeavor—Nahor explored his sexual needs while Sahana explored her body and feminine energy. When the two met, their love making was intense. Neither of them knew where their hearts were going, nor did they understand the meaning of love.

At times she felt she had fallen head over heels for Nahor, but in the back of her mind, she knew that he wasn't worth her feelings. Mentally, she was very strong, but her heart was filled with intense feelings for Nahor. Every time she saw Nahor, she couldn't stop giggling. She often dreamt of a beautiful life with him—their strong love-making sessions, intense conversations, and long walks. She thought her life would be perfect with him. They would make a lovely couple, but that would be too much good fortune in one place. She knew that this dream would never come true. She always knew that the romantic movies that she enjoyed occasionally were only fantasies. Still, she drew pleasure from watching movies and imagining "happily ever after" with her man. She often found herself expressing her feelings on a sheet of paper with vigorous doodles and words that she would read to no one but Nahor. She sent him postcards and letters with excerpts from her diary. She would shed tears all by herself accepting his void in her life, but she never let anyone in her heart. She deeply felt the need of having a man in her life to provide her with security, respect in society, and companionship.

Nahor on the other hand, fell in and out of love. He was so immature that he could hardly ever draw the line between his sexual desires and his feelings of love.

Due to huge debts and issues within her joint family, Sahana and her parents flew out of town. They settled in London, where she further studied trees and attained global fame for her work. Nahor followed her every move and wrote congratulatory emails to her for her achievements. She later got married and joined the State University of Iowa. Within three years of her marriage, she gave birth to two beautiful daughters—Reave and Misty.

Nahor was mentally devastated after Sahana's complete absence from his life. He stopped going to events and eventually made friends with many women he thought he had fallen in love with. Professionally, he worked very hard. He was seen at every global event and was applauded for his extraordinary work on birds. He wrote book after book and won an award for being the youngest writer and achiever by a globally renowned magazine. He later met an interesting woman and married her in order to move on in his life. He had two sons, and he lived happily ever after.

Or so it seemed.

The doctors and businessmen had gathered once again for Nature2001 in Maragoan. But this time, there was a significant departure from their annual gathering. This time, they had raised enough funds to make the event global! They called in experts from all over the world. Given the fame of Sahana and Nahor, not to mention their local roots, the organizers sent an invitation to both of them to conduct a session at the event. They both responded positively.

Sahana and Nahor both flew in. The event was a huge success with a thousand nature enthusiasts learning about various elements of nature in town. When Sahana saw Nahor, she ran into his arms. He almost choked her to death. They stared into each other's eyes like they did when they were younger. They decided to catch up over coffee after a successful event.

Sahana asked for black coffee while Nahor asked for tea. Sahana's skin was still golden brown. When she smiled, the world smiled with her. She had the same beautiful hazel brown eyes that he dreamt of and dark, wavy hair that shone burgundy in the sun. Nahor reminded her that she had Caucasian blood mixed in her family tree. She giggled at that like she always did when he was around.

Nothing had changed between them. Even after years had passed, the bond between them remained as it had been. The desire to make love was still alive. He felt the same tickles in his stomach like he did when he had first met her. Soon they found themselves in his balcony, on the floor, staring into each other's eyes.

Madhushri Mudke is a PhD scholar and writer living in India. She's currently working at the Ashoka Trust for Research in Ecology and the Environment (ATREE), Bangalore. She spends most of her time exploring forests and observing wildlife for her research. When she's back home, in the city, she spends time with her son telling him stories of wild animals and biodiversity. Her work mainly focuses on wildlife, feminism, and scicomm. Occasionally, she finds magic in writing fiction. Find her on social media channels with the handle @girlgonebirdzz

SECTION THREE:

STORIES TO MAKE YOU LAUGH

A Tough Nut to Crack
Dannelle Fraser Gay

How the heck did I get myself into this situation?

I know he started it. This has to be his fault too. Now? I'm just stuck, hanging around, until something changes. I hate this and I feel as if my head is about to explode.

When did this all start?

I know—that stupid bird feeder on a pole! One day, it showed up in my back yard, and it smelled so darned fantastic. That fresh wood smell and the tantalizing aroma of mini nuts. Yup, that was when this all started.

That pole was so easy to climb up—after all, it was just galvanized steel, and I gained traction and momentum quickly as I scaled it. There was literally nothing to a quick hand-hold over the ledge, and I was able to sit at the buffet and shove the birds out of my way.

SUNFLOWER SEEDS!

Oh. My. Stars.

Those are my most *favoritest*. I love to sit up, hold them in both hands, and savor them as I slowly crack open that black and white shell to feast on that mini-nut goodness.

Yup. I hit the motherload.

Until *he* interfered.

Ugh.

Who did he think he was? Putting an upside-down Frisbee just under that buffet to try keeping me out of it?

That didn't last long. After all, I am long, lean, and extremely flexible. Ha! That showed him. I stuck my tongue out at him while he attempted to stare me down through that big shiny hole in the wall of his home. Who doesn't make a home in a tree? Seriously? Never trust a ground-walker.

The next time I went out for a snack? That pole was slippery. It smelled funny too.

Just. *Ick.*

I almost felt like one of those mini-bear thieves. You know, the ones that wear a mask and only come out at night? Those loners hate the feel of anything gooey on their hands, and this jelly-like stuff was simply nasty. We just call them trash pandas.

Which is funny.

He keeps the buffet refills in a silver mini trash can. I can't get it open, even though I can smell the aromatic bounty in there. That trash panda? *She* got into it and knocked it over so the rest of us could indulge too.

That was a good day.

He did something to it though, so even the trash panda couldn't open it again.

I really don't like him.

But I showed him…

Ha!

Buffet for the win! I ate extra just to tick him off and left a little present up there too!

Yup, that was a great day.

Sadly, that gooey substance frustrated me, so I made it a last-ditch plan for my meals. Except for white season. When that white stuff was everywhere, the pole wasn't nearly as slippery or "icky." It was also close, so I hardly had to work or walk for a meal.

Spring came—he must have felt bad. He planted one of my favorite bushes by the buffet. I think it is called a *spiraea prunifolia.*

Keep up with me here: *spiraea prunifolia*, commonly called bridal-wreath spirea or just bridal-wreath, is an upright, clumping, deciduous shrub with arching branches. It typically grows four-to-eight feet tall with a similar spread, often becoming somewhat open and leggy over time. (I have a cousin at the Missouri Botanical Garden that read a plaque about it to me. She's da bomb!)

Bridal-wreath is perfect for my acrobatics. I am still light enough that the branches hold me when I move quickly, and then I can just hop over to the buffet and chow down. It is kind of fun! Well, it was… until he moved it.

Ugh.

No worries, things changed quickly when they added to my yard.

The deck remodel. Be-A-U-T-iful red cedar planks, built-in seats, and even railings. With a slight redwood stain, it was like living in the lap of luxury as I sat upon the railing and ripped into a walnut that I dragged over from the neighbor. Yes, it is more work than the buffet to get into a walnut, but there is a lot of nut inside that shell. I am getting better at it as I get older, I can get more of the nut out with a smaller and smaller hole in the shell. I almost have the perfect spot now to nibble on and take most of the work out of it.

I love my life.

I also left a few presents for him on that railing. Isn't that what smart enemies should do? I like to think of it as a challenge: quit messing with me.

I know he got the message, because he put in a super sun that shines like crazy even in the middle of the night. He must be a really crazy human, as it looks just like the ones out alongside the squirrel killer. I think I heard him tell another human it was a "street right." Yup. You can see that street right, just like it is in the middle of the day. Ugh. It's still a squirrel killer… I have lost more friends to that thing; it just seems to suck the life right out of them and leave them flat!

Anyway, back to that street right. *No more icky stuff!* He was so nice and placed it close to my buffet. I could merely jump to the top of it and then leap over to the buffet.

Once, I missed. Have you ever done that? Ugh, so embarrassing. I managed to turn myself around in midair and land on my feet but had to make it look like I had planned to do that. (whew) I looked around and didn't see anyone watching.

A quick skip, hop, and leap, and I was back to the buffet and holy buckets—he upgraded! Goodbye Sizzler and hello Old Country Buffet. Not only was there an abundance of sunflower seeds but other delectable little nutty goodness. I. Was. In. Heaven.

For a week.

(sigh)

He took away the street right.

Just. Ugh.

I left him numerous presents on his fancy-schmancy deck.

White season came again and then went away. It was a gorgeous spring day, and I was bringing my lady friend over to show her a great time and daze and amaze her with my mad skills. I scrambled up the icky pole and hopped up onto the ledge of the buffet, only to fall down with a small shower of mini nuts. To add insult to injury, I got hit on the head with a small piece of wood.

Ugh.

She was totally watching, and there was no way I could brush it off as a planned activity.

(sigh)

She almost passed out laughing.

Somehow, I get the feeling that she isn't the right mother for my kits.

I have no idea how long she laughed at me because I went to the next yard that had the walnuts. See if I share with her again.

Ugh.

The next day I went back to see what the damage really was to my buffet.

Eek!

It was *gone*—pole and all.

Where it had been was a small pile of dirt in the ground and a few scattered mini nuts.

I could cry.

But wait. I saw something out of the corner of my eye. It looked like another buffet? But it wasn't on a pole, and it hung from some kind of shiny ropes off his land house. Right in front of that big shiny hole in the wall of his home. He must really want to keep an eye on it.

How…

How could I get to it?

I had to think about this. It took me three days, but I came up with a plan (That will show him!).

If I climb up the seven-foot wooden fence, I could run along the top of it. I would have to jump over those stupid spears that are every six feet or so. Seriously? Design choices are almost endless. If he wanted to add a finishing touch to the top of his fence posts, he could have picked anything else and made my life easier, not to mention make the fence look better. Now? I have to look like a bad impersonation of Donkey Kong as I race along the fence.

The fence will take me to the apricot tree. I know for a fact that he has never harvested an apricot because I pull them off before they are orange. I kind of like the green ones—ha! Anyway, the apricot tree takes me to the tall pine tree. I can jump from that, to the next one, to the next one, to the next one, until I get to his ground house. I will be on top of it.

Then I would have to get to the edge. Easy-peasy. There is that rain-catching trough that fits my fanny perfectly. It has a few spots where I can get a good grip and work my way down to that shiny rope that holds my buffet.

Let's do this.

Climb the fence, run along the top, jump, run, jump, run, jump, run, jump, run, jump, run, jump, run, jump to the apricot tree. Jump to the pine tree. Jump to the next pine tree. Jump to the next pine tree. Jump to the next pine tree. Jump to his house. Crawl down the roof to the rain catcher. Climb down that shiny rope.

Crap.

Did anyone see that? I looked around and didn't see anyone watching (whew).

Let me look at it again...

Aha! There are holes in it. I am an acrobat. I can *do* this.

I leaned over the edge of the rain catcher, wrapped my hands around it, flipped my behind over the edge, and got my back feet on it. I weaved my back feet in its links and then, once I felt secure, bent over backwards to reach down into the buffet and eat my fill.

SUNFLOWER SEEDS!

Oh. My. Stars.

A Tough Nut to Crack　∾　Dannelle Fraser Gay

Did I tell you that those are my most favoritest?

There were tons of them on the buffet! All that mini-nut goodness literally at the tips of my fingers.

I ate a lot (burp).

Which leads me to my current problem… How the heck did I get myself into this situation? I know he started it. This has to be his fault too. Now? I'm just stuck, hanging around, until something changes. I hate this and I feel as if my head is about to explode.

He's getting another present.

∾

Published author, public speaker, and mom of an amazing kid … Dannelle has been hopping the globe for more than thirty years to indulge in fun food, activities, and adventures while writing for websites and books.

With a penchant for creative storytelling and living a champagne life on a beer budget, she keeps beyond busy with her laptop.

Get more of Dannelle at www.DannelleFraserGay.com *or one of Southern Wisconsin's news outlets as she has been seen on* NBC15, CBS3, Mom's Everyday, Wisconsin Public Radio, Wisconsin State Journal, *etc.*

STOLEN MOMENT
LINNÉ ELIZABETH

I stole the truck.

The thought echoed in Miranda's mind as she slammed her palms on the steering wheel, emphasizing each unspoken word. It should have been easy. Get in. Take the nav system, headlights, and anything else valuable. Get out.

The sirens' squeals receded as she sped down the street toward the orb of lights guiding her to City Center. She pressed down on the accelerator with a white-knuckle grip on the leather-covered wheel to rush through a yellow light. It turned red as she sped through the intersection—another broken law to add to her rap sheet.

A plan. She needed a plan. Get far out of the city and ditch the truck. She could target another F-250—she'd have to. A red light flashed in her peripheral. A surge of panic jump-started her heart as she jerked the steering wheel to the right. The truck plowed through a narrow one-way street enclosed on either side by towering redbrick buildings. With another decisive turn, she pulled the truck into an open service bay. The steep incline hid the F-250 from view.

Throwing the rig into park, she slunk down in the soft seat and held her breath. No wail of sirens. No flashing red-and-blue lights. She expelled her breath like an over-filled balloon. Her heart slowed to match her measured breaths.

Leaning against the headrest, she closed her eyes—the anxiety of the chase melted into fear. Forgiveness wasn't Slade's thing. It didn't matter that Trevy bolted at the first note of the sirens' wailing. Slade would task her with siphoning gas as punishment. Miranda's mouth puckered at the memory of the bitter burn. Getting caught might be the better option.

A white light illuminated the interior of the truck. Tires screeched. Miranda's slight frame wrenched forward like a rag doll and then thrust back by what felt like the pressure of a cinder block.

She sat, cemented to the seat while the airbag deflated. Gasping for air, she pushed the gauzy material away from her body. Fine dust coated her lungs, sending her into a coughing fit. The driver's door creaked open.

"Hey! Hey! You okay?"

Miranda blinked her eyes to clear her vision from the powder assault of the airbag. A set of grease-covered hands reached in and undid her seat belt.

"Um, I think so." Her body ached, and her lungs burned, but she would keep that to herself. This do-gooder couldn't call the police or an ambulance. "I'm fine. Great, actually." She rolled out of the driver's seat with the grace of a drunk sorority girl. Her feet hit the pavement, legs wobbling, but she remained upright.

Miranda faced her rescuer. He was taller than her with an athletic build. Even with him wearing a mechanic's jumper, she could make out his muscular body. Chestnut hair framed his oval face. He twisted a maroon shop rag in hands that looked better suited to playing the piano than working on an engine. He stooped down to catch her. A silver hoop glinted on his arched eyebrow as he leaned closer to her.

She should say something. "Look. I appreciate your help, but I'm okay. So … we don't need to call anyone about this." She pointed to the Suburban that rammed the truck so hard it had crumpled the bed into an accordion.

He exhaled and stuffed the rag in his back pocket. "Thank you, Jesus!" He pulled a cross from the chain around his neck and kissed it once while staring toward the sky. "I can take care of this. All this." He passed her a small, square black card. In a flourished scroll, it read: The Mechanic, contact@themechanic.com

Her lips twitched into a slight smile at its nondescript and mysterious nature. "Catchy."

He ran a hand through his thick hair and laughed, such a joyful sound Miranda's breath hitched. She wanted to hear it again.

100

"Yeah, well, it's what my friends call me. I can fix your truck. Good as new." Miranda slipped the black card in her jacket pocket. She didn't need the truck fixed. She needed to deliver parts to Slade. A fresh wave of fear roiled in the pit of her stomach. Slade knew how to hold a grudge. The sooner she got another truck, the better.

The driver's seat of the Suburban was empty. "So, where's the idiot who hit me?"

The mechanic stuck his hands in the pockets of the coveralls and looked to the ground. Miranda nodded. "Oh. You're the idiot. Didn't you see my brake lights?"

His eyes met hers. "Not until I turned. It was too late." Then his eyes narrowed. "But what exactly are you doing parked in *my* service bay at 3 a.m.?"

Cornered by the question, Miranda stepped back from him. The world shifted, and Miranda's body went with it. The Mechanic caught her and eased her down to the pavement. Wrapped in the scent of engine oil and sandalwood, she mumbled, "No doctors."

He nodded and didn't move her except to relax into a seated position. She molded into his lap, soaking in the heat between their bodies.

"So, what's a girl like you doing in a truck like this?"

The muscles in her arms tensed. "Girls can't drive trucks?"

He shrugged. "Most city girls don't."

"I'm not most girls."

"No, you're not." Miranda could hear the smile on his face. She shifted to see him better. His lips turned up into a sexy side smile. Heat ran the length of her body. "You just don't seem like the truck type of girl."

The warm sensation turned to ice. She scrambled off his lap. He knew what she'd done. What if Slade sent him? She didn't know all of Slade's lackeys. She needed to get the truck out now. "You're right. Uh, it's not mine. I actually ... need to get it back."

The Mechanic quirked his head and studied her like she was one puzzle piece shy of a complete picture.

Sealing her mouth shut against any lies that could complicate matters, she smiled at him. Slade's voice filled her mind: *Only say enough to lead him to his own conclusions.*

The Mechanic slapped his legs and stood up. "All right. Well, I've got a friend with a tow truck. I'll text him, and we can get 'not your truck' back to my shop. Unless you wanted to return it like this?"

He drifted back toward the Suburban. Miranda enjoyed the view for a moment before nausea forced her to place her head between her legs.

Breathing in her nose and out her mouth seemed to keep the dizzy spell in check enough to run inventory on the job that was dissolving into a nightmare. The front of the Ford F-250 rammed the service bay door, but the bumper might be okay. Headlights were a loss, but the nav system might be salvageable. Wheels were still a viable option.

A shuffle signaled the Mechanic's return. He crouched next to her. "He'll be here in ten." Sirens echoed in the distance.

Miranda's heart froze. She swallowed the impulse to run, doubtful that she'd make it very far in her current state.

The Mechanic swore in a hushed whisper.

She glared at him. "We agreed."

His hands shot up in the air, pleading innocence. "I didn't call them."

A charcoal-colored Escalade pulled behind the Suburban. Three additional squad cars boxed in the service bay.

She slumped down to the ground. "Slade's gonna kill me."

The lights bathed the Mechanic's face in alternating shades of blue and red. "The truck owner?"

She shook her head. It didn't matter if he knew the truth now. The cops found her. In a matter of seconds, they'd cuff her and haul her away. Clearing her throat, she forced her voice to be strong. "My boss, who's expecting parts from that F-250."

The Mechanic's mouth fell open. He laughed, but this time Miranda didn't enjoy the resonant sound. She narrowed her eyes at his reaction.

He was laughing so hard tears spilled from the corner of his eyes. He wiped them, leaving a trail of grease smudges on his cheeks. "You *stole* the F-250? No fuc—."

"Down on your knees. Place your hands behind your head." A crackling voice called over a loudspeaker.

Miranda was plenty capable of stealing cars. Well, parts from trucks. Except for tonight. This pretty boy didn't deserve an explanation. His body convulsed with barely contained laughter. She scowled at the Mechanic as she pushed off the pavement.

With small precise strokes, she brushed the dirt from her hands. They would strip the freedom of movement from her soon, and having dirt-covered hands was an unnecessary discomfort. She sighed and knelt, one knee at a time. Small rocks dug through the paper-thin leggings. The Mechanic mirrored her movements with an aftershock of chuckles quaking his frame.

Six inky silhouettes eased forward in the blinding spotlights. Two broke off for Miranda and pulled her up from the ground. Adrenaline pumped through her limbs, masking her pain and nausea. A lanky officer slapped cuffs on Miranda's wrist. The icy metal bit into her skin.

She shivered while his fairylike partner chirped: "You may remain silent, anything you say…"

Miranda tuned it out. The Mechanic was no longer laughing; instead, he knelt in front of four captors of his own. The cuffs had warmed on her skin, and while Officer Stringbean had been gentle, the metal on her skin rubbed. Her wrist would be raw by the time processing was over.

"Well?" The female officer stood waiting with a pen hovering over a notepad. Did she expect a confession? Slade's advice sounded again: *Keep your cool. Cops never know anything.* In a voice more confident than she felt, she responded, "Well, what?"

Officer Stringbean exchanged a charged look with his partner. Then he repeated the question like he was talking to a toddler. "Are you working with Mateo?"

Miranda didn't need to fake confusion. "Who's Mateo?"

Officer Stringbean pointed to the Mechanic.

His partner sighed as if put out by this arrest. "Are you working for him?"

Miranda shook her head. "I'm not a mechanic."

She scoffed. "Neither is he."

Officer Stringbean's chuckle cut short at Miranda's glare. He adjusted his belt and composed himself. "Mateo runs a chop shop out in Central."

Miranda's mouth fell open. They were here for *him*.

Mateo's hazel eyes met Miranda's. He winked before being shoved into the back of the squad car.

*   *   *

Miranda stepped out the door of the county jail and into the warm sunlight. Six months gone. Lucky as she was to get a lawyer who made a case for joyriding, she still lost six months of her life. Treading down the pathway toward the closest bus stop, each step sapped a little more of her confidence. Slade always cut his losses. Once a person went down, he didn't accept failure, but he might take her back.

Pulling off her jacket, she crossed the parking lot and paused. Leaning against the hood of a fully restored Chevy Impala, she saw him. Complete with a cocky smirk, Mateo, aka the Mechanic, pulled off his aviator sunglasses and waved like they were old friends.

She shook her head and sauntered up to him with as much gusto as any girl could after getting out of jail. "You stole the Suburban."

"Nothing gets past you."

She rolled her eyes. "You ran into a parked truck."

He looked to the ground, kicked at the gravel, and nodded. "Turns out I'm better in the shop."

She folded her arms over her chest. "Well, I'm better at lifting parts."

He glanced at her through a full set of lashes and smiled. "I've got a proposition." She walked around the Impala, dragging one finger along the body. "What's that?" The look in his eyes promised mischief. "Dinner?"

She pulled the driver's side door open and sat down. "You're paying."

∾

Linne Elizabeth is a freelance content writer by day and fiction writer by night. Her short stories are featured in multiple anthologies and online magazines. When she's not earning money, developing twisted plotlines for short stories, or wrestling with edits of her first novel, you can find her playing in the rust-colored desert of Southern Utah with her incredible (sometimes feral) kids and her handsome and supportive husband. Check her out on Instagram: @library4one *or on Facebook:* @linneelizabeth

THE RECITAL
WADE FRANSSON

My childhood was tumultuous, to say the least, and it left me searching for answers. In response, I applied to and was eventually accepted to a Bible college operated by a Christian fundamentalist sect called The Worldwide Church of God. I enrolled in January, moving from a frigid and remote Anchorage, Alaska, to a hot and cosmopolitan Pasadena, California. During my first twelve months there, I was transformed. Infused with a moral compass, spirituality, and a hefty dose of self-righteousness, I considered myself in many ways superior to those around me—both inside the school and among the broader community outside of it.

These feelings were validated and heightened as I approached the conclusion of my third semester. Herbert Armstrong, Founder of the Worldwide Church of God, then in his eighties, announced me as one of seventy students selected to transfer to the newly reopened Big Sandy, Texas campus—which was offering two-year associate degrees. Mr. Armstrong personally spoke at an assembly to encourage us to reestablish this sister campus of God's college and teach the incoming freshmen God's way. I was also chosen to be an Ambassador Club President, cementing my status as a student leader.

As if that weren't enough, I was also selected to participate in one of the college's premier summer opportunities—on "the Dig"—the prestigious archaeological excavation at Jerusalem's City of David, sponsored by Hebrew University. I would visit family in Sweden, where I had spent almost three years as a child, and travel through Europe before meeting the group in Athens.

From there, we would embark on a boat ride to Haifa and our tour of duty in the Holy Land.

Therefore, it should come as no surprise that I established myself, over my year at the Texas campus—in the eyes of many students and faculty in Big Sandy—as a pompous, self-righteous, wanna-be minister.

This was not entirely fair, as my actual focus was self-improvement and pleasing my Creator. In keeping with this goal, I decided to address my past affection for "the devil's music" by joining the choir and enrolling in piano classes. This was my first-ever attempt to play an instrument. I was an absolute beginner in a group of students who had been playing since preschool. My insecurities had previously led me to strictly avoid such situations. Still, in this safe environment, my embarrassment was manageable right up until the mandatory year-end recital. I was assigned two pieces: a Czechoslovakian children's ditty and a beginner's duet with the teacher, Mrs. Bryant.

The dress was semi-formal, and surrounding dignitaries were invited to this East Texas cultural highlight. Dressed up, everyone displayed their snootiest behavior—which for the WCG, especially AC—is saying a lot. I was the last to perform before the intermission. Several accomplished performers had already played to an enthusiastic audience when I confidently walked on stage to announce my two simple pieces. I took care to articulate the correct pronunciation of the title of the Czechoslovak tune, translating it as "Dance," and announced that I would then play a duet with Mrs. Bryant. I sat down and managed my way through "Dance" while the audience looked puzzled and exchanged first confused, then knowing glances.

Mrs. Bryant then joined me on the piano bench. I paused briefly before dramatically banging out three alternating chords in 4/4 rhythm. Mrs. Bryant commenced her light, lively melody on the upper keys, and I smiled, as the effect was pleasant and actually entertaining. I missed one of the chords badly on my second attempt, resulting in a loud, discordant noise, followed by a repressed laugh from Dominick Furlano, who was sitting in the second row. Having let the first laugh go, he could not stop himself from continuing. As his muffled giggles grew louder, it was time for my third round of chords. The same wrong chord rang out above the exploding laughter, as others failed in their desperate efforts not to join him. After I vigorously banged out the wrong chord for the third time, the entire audience was in hysterics.

Mrs. Bryant, seated between the audience and me, recognized a hopeless situation and stood to bow. But I grabbed her left sleeve with my right hand and pulled her down on the seat, determined to finish the song. The audience howled uncontrollably as I massacred my part for a fourth time. Poor, sweet, demure Mrs. Bryant could no longer contain herself, and her hands left the keyboard to cover her mouth. In contrast to Dominick and most of the audience, she attempted to restrain her laughter, but her petite body betrayed her by bouncing like a Mexican jumping bean on the piano bench next to me.

By now, Dominick had literally fallen off his chair into the aisle, and someone stood up to lead the audience in applause to put an end to my merciless humiliation. I had succeeded in bringing an entire audience to a hysterical standing ovation—laughing not *with* me but at me. There were a few who were not laughing; they were in shock at what they assumed might be causing permanent damage to my tender ego.

Even as we took our bows and left the stage, the laughter still overpowered the applause, and intermission was called, during which the audience discussed loudly what they had just experienced. Rather than being crushed, the effect on me was liberating. Bringing the house down with my incompetence was cathartic. The distance between others and me would never again be quite as great.

The overall effect of my year in Big Sandy was to breakdown some of the defenses I had built to protect myself, allowing me to become just a little bit more human as a result. With the barriers coming down, I began to worry less about self-justification and self-righteousness and began, ever so slowly, to realize that the person in front of me was more important than whatever was going on inside my head.

∾

Wade Fransson's life journey has taken him all over the world, and provided him with compelling philosophical and spiritual insights.

After a troubled childhood involving divorce, domestic kidnapping, and an international custody battle, Wade joined, and later became a minister in the Worldwide Church of God. He shared this in his stirring autobiographical story across the volumes "The People of the Sign" and "The Hardness of the Heart." Wade decided to found a publishing company, which he did in 2012. While on a 2014 trip to India to receive a lifetime achievement award, as a keynote speaker at a series of conferences in Chennai, inaugurated by the governor of Tamil Nadu, he gained in prayer, the answer to a Biblical questions that prompted the mind-expanding and satisfying conclusions to his Trilogy, in the third volume – "The Rod of Iron."

Along the way, Wade has also pursued teaching at the elementary school level, earned an MBA and held significant roles in noteworthy companies. He also established a successful business services company and later co-founded the Internet Startup GoHuman.com, before founding Something Or Other Publishing *with its* Royal Falcon Imprint. *Wade currently lives in Madison, Wisconsin with his wife and their two children.*

STORIES TO HELP YOU IMAGINE THE POSSIBILITIES

THE BALLAD OF IS'ADORA
A.M. MAC HABEE

The last sun was setting when she strolled up to the tavern. Its thick wooden walls were painted with green and yellow flowers. Its door was bright red with a notice nailed to it; a curfew from the mayor.

"So," she said, straightening, "three have died here already."

Inside, it stank of stale ale, vomit, urine, and a subtle undercurrent of spice. Patrons continued to crowd the poorly lit tables; their hard, dirty hands gripped the uneven clay of their shallow mugs. Some were missing limbs. They had no intentions of leaving soon.

It's the perfect venue, thought Is'adora, as she made her way to the platform and began to tune the lute.

The owner gave her a slight nod and continued to serve his customers. Bards were good for business, and for the last couple of weeks, Is'adora had seen no other bard.

Some children played by the nearby fire's light. Their wooden toys were chipped and broken. Their clothes were little more than ill-fitted rags.

It would be light on coin, but taverns often let the bard stay the night and offered them food too. It was enough to please Is'adora. She was, after all, only a few days away from her destination.

After her lute was perfectly tuned, she played a simple opening harmony.

> *Thalians do gather around, I pluck strings,*
> *To a tale of Queens and of Kings,*
> *Who abandoned the gods and destroyed themselves.*
> *"The Dance that Ended the Yellow Elves"*

The Ballad of Is'adora ∽ A.M. Mac Habee

The ballad was short, especially her version, but the pretense was enough. The children gathered by her feet, and a few patrons lazily glanced up from their mugs.

Gods, please spare my life, I won't prolong
my tale, for I'm guided by the Goddess of Music.
Silta, protect my tongue, fingers, and lyric.
I use them to worship you every day with my song.
Please do not harm my fine audience,
They are honest and laborious,
who break their bodies opening the soil,
for Sol and Eh'colte gods of harvest and toil.

She changed the rhythm, for the tale was about to begin.
To the east on the isle of Creten, over one thousand years hence,
when giants still lived, when the gods would condense
into mortal shells, concealed as us.
The year Hi'lak slew hordes of Treehous.
Yellow Elf eyes were springtime flowers
Their hair was so golden it made queens cower,
Their skin was sunlight, and their lips were fire.
Their heavy feet would sink in any quagmire.
They were most beloved by the Goddess Fu'rnac,
ruler of the flame, patron of the furnace,
mother of dragons, with the coldest embrace.
Strands of her hair forged their race.
The greed of goblins, who treasured their hair,
plucked their eyes for ointments, tore skin for chairs.
After thirty decades, they were aghast.
For the Yellow Elves of Creten were the last.

* * *

Queen, Se'Caite, died on the last day of summer.
They mourned two hundred days, and from her
Tomb, daughter Se'liah, was crowned queen.
Wearing a Godly forged crown for all to be seen.
Her people, awestruck, cried, "Two hundred more!"
"Two hundred more!" For she was so adored.
That night she hid in her mother's old bed chamber,
Enraptured by their memories, none could blame her.
On the morrow, her eyes were still wide with shock,
A scream never heard; the door still locked.
And in the suns' light, she was cold to the touch,
White sheets crimson, the crown grasped in her clutch.
There was a squeal of delight from all but one of the children.

The lyrics fell from Is'adora's lips, the tempo slowed, and the notes trailed. Hearing the strange shift, the patrons stiffened in their seats and began to look around at each other, like a peculiar haze had suddenly lifted from them.

A kingdom must have a ruler, the gods themselves decided so.
Without an Heir Apparent, the council turned to her brother,
Se'laphiz. If crowned, the first king to sit the throne in three thousand years.
A king from which the land would never recover.
He denied her rites as a fallen queen.
Instead electing that her corpse be sealed,
In their mother's tomb. From womb to grave, she was just sixteen.
Only ten days later, his grief had healed.
During those ten days, the palace maids scrubbed,
they polished,
they buffed and did all but scrape it off.
But there was no use.
On the eleventh day, Se'laphiz was crowned king.
But his crown, forged by the gods, was blemished.

The golden metal was speckled with small red dots,
The white gem at its top, which once caught the radiant light of
the three suns,
was now blood red.
its dark hue absorbed all light that touched it,
and kept it for its own.

Is'adora blinked rapidly, shook her long, green hair, and took up her tune again.

The best wine from Bezat, the Mage Kingdom,
meat from Solun, tastiest and most seldom,
fruit from the Forest Kingdom, gathered by Fae.
From Kingdoms Lut, silk with the richest dye.

The people's eyes widened. Just one of these luxuries was worth more than all their lifetime earnings combined.

Jewels from Therak, a bounty so plentiful,
their castle, built from crystal, was a skull,
that watched their people flourish. Spice,
from Thalia, the finest flavors to entice.

A cheer rang out through the Tavern as mugs clunked together.
Gold thread weaved from their brimful island mines,
hard sewn kingly outfits were redesigned.
"We will make merry for one thousand years!"
Declared the king of fleshly pleasures, cheers!
They danced until they could no longer walk,
indulged 'til Fu'nac's offerings were forgotten.
Instead of in the temple, in stoppers as hogs,
no more worshipers or thanks to the gods.
Who made the world, animals, stars, and food,

to Fu'rnac who weaved them all, now screwed,
as her hurt pulled her down from the sky,
disguised as a young woman, destined to die.

Is'adora's olive skin speckled with brown, her viridescent eyes narrowed, and her teeth locked. She held the terrified lute as if one more note would break it.

She entered the castle through a haze of smoked root,
sticky wine covered the floor, her gaze astute.
As around her bodies contort, groaning.
No mortal noticed as she went for the king.
"Your Royal Highness," she knelt before him,
seated, he ripped shreds from the carcass,
his greasy mouth sucked the sticky limb.
"My lord, today is the Furltane Festival,
to pay homage to Fu'rnac, the ineffable,
where are the offerings? The flurry
of worshipers? The songs of her glory?"
He took a swig of wine to clear his throat,
"There will be no offerings, no worship, and no songs of glory,
other than the glory of merriment and cheer.
For every day with me as king is a day to celebrate."
"Are you saying that you should be celebrated,
but the gods should not?"
"We have worshiped for many years,
Surely they must be tired of it by now."
He began to eat again, and the Fu'rnac sizzled under her cloak.
While his mouth overflowed with meat, the king added,
"Perhaps if they did something new, we would worship them more.
Until then,
we will dance until the ground shakes, until the world throws itself
at my feet."
Fu'rnac seethed, "But what about the goddess who made you?"
He gave a hearty laugh and spat at the stranger before him.

"But what about the king who provides you with all?"
The court laughed until the whole room shook.
Fu'rnac departed enraged, such mortal gall,
their ancient goddess, they had forsaken.
At the highest peak of the mountainous island,
Fu'rnac crouched down; her mortal shell tore.
The flesh caught fire, burned away.
The goddess's red eyes glared at the castle as she bore down.
And from within her came an egg of molten fire.
She held it to her chest and whispered,
"I name you Vo'l, child of Fu'rnac.
One day you and your children will cover the earth.
Your glowing arms will spread wide.
Your booming voice will break stone.
Your dark breath will consume all light.
You will hatch when they dance until the ground shakes,
You will throw the world at their feet,
and bury them with it."
She hid the egg under the island and fizzled into vapor.

Someone passed Is'adora an ale, and she tipped it up, letting the ale pour down her shirt.

"Thank you, kind sir! Now, are you all ready for a little romance?" The crowd awkwardly cheered, and the little girls made disgusted faces.

The youngest royal daughters sent as brides,
The King of Creten lent back sighed.
He turned half away on the first night,
ages varied, and they weren't very bright.
Then he quickly turned away twenty more,
they were devout, and his wife will worship him alone,
then there remained three to adore.
One princess fair and rich would share his throne.

No'litha, from the kingdom of spices fine
Li'ts, the blue princess of silks sublime.
Finally, Wo'th, who carried wine-red swords.
He would have chosen wine, 'til spice sang to birds.

*   *   *

After a decade, people had grown,
weary of celebration, yet they continued.
No'litha declared a queen of their own
will arrive, and new laws should be issued.
To slow the incredible import of goods,
worship gods again, "Thank them for our heir."
A safe, happy place for future childhoods,
A sturdy kingdom for their daughter's care.
The king looked upon his wife, his love,
and cupped her face in his hand's soft curve.
After a few moments, he told his choice,
"Anything for you 'Litha, be consoled."
"Grant me one night to celebrate our child.
The biggest party the world has ever seen.
They will stop, the last occasion to be wild,
A kingdom she'd be proud to be queen."
He kissed her tenderly, flooded with tears
As he caressed her belly, filled with answered prayers.
Fu'rnac had been waiting for just such a moment,
And gathered gods to bear witness.

Is'adora built her crescendo with a foreboding tune.

Creten danced as if it were the first night.
For the queen was pregnant, and the revelries
would end. Music swelled through the streets, alleys,

masking birds' squawks of terror as they took flight.
"My love," Se'laphiz whispered, "Let's dance for the last time,
before our child graces us with her shine."
The child rolled over, painfully shoving,
but she could refuse her lover nothing.
The baby kicked harder in her womb.
Sensing a heat that would be their doom.
The buildings swayed with the royal couple.
Their dance ending as the walls crumbled.
Great waves battered the shoreline.
Buildings fell as people fled to the sea,
only to find it flooded by giant waves,
their boats smashed apart into battered debris.
From deep beneath them, an egg cracked,
with a boom that was heard across every land.
Dark smoke filled the sky and their lungs,
no screams were heard from blackened tongues.
The king clutched his queen, her face pained,
as Vo'l's glowing arms lifted the earth
the land rent asunder during his birth.
The waters gushed in the broken ring that remained.
The grave of five hundred-thousand, the end of their skin.
It wasn't just the birthplace of Vo'l, but its kin.
And if you visit the Island, you will see
they stand screaming, encased in rock for eternity.

Only the children clapped in the last rays of sunlight as the day faded into a pale pink and bright orange. Taking their cue, the adults swallowed their remaining ale and paid Is'adora a few coppers. She watched them leave. Her dark, red eyes flashed in her mortal shell as the townsfolk mumbled about how they had never heard a stranger tune and how some of the details were new, like the queen's baby. Fu'rnac couldn't blame them. She wasn't Silta, after all.

AM Mac Habee is an award-winning artist and published author born in Montreal, Canada, to a shy program architect and the wild Australian that stole his heart. AM lives in a small bungalow tucked away in a seaside corner of England's Northeast with two working cats, a gestating daughter, and a dedicated husband who works full-time as AM's caregiver. As a non-binary, pansexual, and disabled person, their writing— whether it be fiction, non-fiction or academic—will often reflect intersectional issues that impact their daily life. After graduating from the University of Ottawa with a Distinction BA in English Literature, AM developed a particular interest in multi-media visual arts, interdisciplinary collaborations and the limits of literary forms. Following this, their current studies toward their MA in Creative Writing at Durham University has led to an even greater interest in form, how it can be bent and how it can be broken.

OF QUESTS, FIREFIGHTERS, AND RELUCTANT WITCHES

J.M. RHINEHEART

When the first knight came through, Millie thought it was a joke. She wasn't exactly a witch in a swamp anymore—she had a chalkboard with specials, and she closed at nine in the evening. Her worst enemy was the distributor, who, currently, owed her a huge shipment of books and was trying to stiff her the late shipping fees. She didn't *do* quests anymore. And whatever quest someone was on, there was the internet to help them.

Those facts didn't stop the man from coming in—clad in thick armor with a sword strapped to his side and storming straight up to her counter. A handful of customers gave him quick looks, but most ignored him. After all, it was faire season, and Millie already had a few customers dressed as jesters and fairies scattered throughout the bookstore. It was probably why she didn't really pay attention at first.

"What can I get you?" she asked him.

He narrowed his gaze at her. "Are you the witch I must seek my quest from?"

Millie's eyebrows went to her hairline. "Seek your quest from? Is that your way of saying you want me to choose your drink for you?" This was going to be a task and a half.

"No, not that," he said in frustration. "I mean *the* quest."

She paused, hands tightening around the keyboard. "I don't have anything related to quests at this time," she said after a moment. "But there's plenty of medieval texts in the back."

His face twisted with evident frustration. "I was told that you were the witch I needed to seek out the missing princess," he said. "My quest is simple but necessary. If you cannot help me, then I'll go elsewhere."

He stormed out then, boots and sword clanging, and slammed the door so hard behind him that she winced. A few customers spared him glances then returned to their drinks and books.

It couldn't be a real quest. It just couldn't. This wasn't Europe in the 700s, this was modern America, and she had free Wi-Fi available to customers. That was as close to magic as she got these days. And a princess?

It had to be a joke. It had to be. There were days that she loved the Renaissance Faire a few miles down the road from Middleton, and then there were days that they were a downright nuisance.

She shrugged it off and turned to her next customer with a smile. "What can I get you?"

*　*　*

When the second knight came through, he was far subtler than the first, dressed in leggings and a leather vest. His sword was by his side, and he carried an ax on his opposite hip.

It was late enough that, thankfully, he wasn't going to cause a ruckus, even with that amount of weaponry on him. Still, she was near to closing, and she wanted to be done for the night.

"We close in ten," she told him.

"I have questions to ask of you, oh, witch of knowledge," he said. "I'm on a quest where time is of the essence."

Millie crossed her arms over her chest and scowled at him. "I don't help people on quests," she said. "Self-help section is all the way to the back and on the right."

"This is not a joke," the man said, glaring at her. "I beseech you to aid me! A princess's life is on the line!"

His hands reached for his hips, and Millie instinctively felt her own hands tighten into fists. She hadn't conjured up anything in more than seventy years, but she'd manage if it came to it. He wasn't going to hurt her or any of her customers, and he sure as hell wasn't going to damage the display she'd just set up at the counter.

But he only settled his hands on his hips and huffed at her. "If you shall not help me, I'll find her on my own," he snapped, and he tore off for the door. This time, the door rattled ominously when he slammed it shut, and she wondered if she ought to tape it to protect it from future angry knights.

She rolled her eyes and turned back to pulling the last of the baked goods out from the counter. There weren't going to be any other knights, she decided. There was no need to fortify her shop. They wouldn't be bothering her again anytime soon.

And she didn't do quests anymore. She hadn't done them in nearly five hundred years; she wasn't about to break her own vow and start again.

* * *

The third knight came the next day. The fourth knight came two days after that. The fifth and sixth knights both came the day after that within twenty minutes of each other.

By the time the door opened on the seventh day, and a large man stepped through, eyes instantly locking on her, Millie was beyond done with the whole thing.

"What?" she snapped.

He cautiously moved up to the counter, eyes going from her to the board behind her. "Um, how about an espresso with some hazelnut syrup?"

Oh. "Sorry," she said, cheeks flushing. "Give me five. In a to-go cup or a mug?"

"Mug, please." He glanced at the case. "Is that an orange scone?"

"Made fresh every morning," she said, already pounding the espresso grounds into place. "Pastries are two for six dollars."

"Then I'll take two."

Glass shot under the spout; she began gathering the pastries together. "Sorry again," she apologized, placing the scones on a plate. "It's been a week."

"I can see that," he said with a grin. It faded slightly as he pulled out a piece of paper. "Does it have anything to do with this?"

Hesitantly she took it and glanced it over. Her eyes widened at the delicate script and the words scrawled on it.

He that can read this
Hath been called upon
To rescue the maiden princess
From the clutches of an evil one
Whose darkness dares to defy light.
Delay not in your questing
Seek the witch within the village
Whose cat holds many tales
And receive the first step
To rescue the maiden and thy bounty.

"Hemlock," she cursed. Well, that explained her visitors over the past week. They hadn't really known she was a witch, but with a name like *The Black Cat Bookshop*, well, it was clear where they were being directed to.

"I figured," the man said. "To be honest, I ... thought it was a joke."

She took a better look at him. He was clearly no longer in uniform, but she could smell something that was distinctly smoky in nature, and his t-shirt gave him away. "Station 205," she said. "You're not far from here."

"I've been meaning to come in here for a while, but I haven't had the chance yet," he said. "Ever since I transferred over, all the people at the station rave about your coffee and keep telling me to get my ass over here." He nodded to the paper. "I figured that was some sort of silly invitation, but one look at your face said it's not."

"It's not," she agreed. "I don't know what's going on, but you're not the first one here for it." The paper didn't look old, but the script looked familiar. Why did it look familiar?

"Lance."

She glanced up out of her wonderings and found his hand stretched over the counter. "Oh! Sorry. I'm Millie." His hand engulfed hers, and she absently wondered if he was a half-giant. No, just someone who'd probably played football in high school and who definitely would've made Arthur's list for knighthood.

She finished up his drink, her eyes going back to the paper. It had to do with the "t". There was something about each t that pulled at her. The loop, the angular hook at the end: where had she seen it last?

"So, um. Should I be calling my friend Arthur?"

She blinked. "What?"

"Arthur," Lance said, waving the paper up. "Captain with the local PD? With another possible missing person?"

Oh, that Arthur. His kids were sweethearts, and his wife was always waiting on the next romance novel. "Maybe," she said. "I honestly don't know how serious to take that. Without anything else, Art is probably going to have to toss it." Though he'd be happy to have something to do. The best and worst thing about sleepy towns was that there usually wasn't much for a police captain to do outside of traffic tickets and the occasional cat up a tree.

Then she stopped. "Wait. *Another* possible missing person? Who else is missing?"

"Some teen girl," Lance said. "Uh, Elizabeth Merrano, I think. Her mom said she's visiting a friend for a few weeks before school starts, and she hasn't heard from her like she was supposed to. Arthur kinda put it on the back burner." He raised an eyebrow. "Art, huh?"

"Don't tell him I said that," Millie warned him, but her gaze went distant. Elizabeth came to the shop every now and then as a children's-time reader. The kids loved her, especially when…

A cold chill ran up her spine. "Hellebore," she muttered. Lance frowned, clearly confused, and she let out a sigh. "Elizabeth reads for the kids every now and then, but she's most known for dressing up and reading as a princess."

Lance didn't need any time to put two and two together and come up with, *Oh crap.* "Guess his suspected missing person is about to become a real missing person," Lance said grimly. "I think I need that coffee to go."

25 Servings of SOOP

"I think I need my associate to handle things," Millie said. "Because I'm coming with you." For whatever reason, she was wrapped up in this, and if she could help a child get home, then she was going to do it.

Then find out who had sent the missives and hex them. Hard. Because there was no way they weren't involved in Elizabeth's disappearance.

*　*　*

Between the letter and Millie's story about the numerous men coming in and inquiring about their quest for a princess, that was more than enough evidence for Art. "I'll get one of my guys over to the faire, see if someone's leaving those papers there," he said. "If you get any others in, call me. Better than that, call the officer sitting outside your place."

"There's an officer outside my shop?" Millie asked, a bit incredulous.

"No, but there's going to be," Arthur said firmly. "Whatever this is, you're being tagged as part of it, and I don't need two people missing in whatever game this psycho has going."

There wasn't much that Millie could do to argue with that, and it would be nice to have someone keeping an eye on the shop, if just for the sake of her two part-time employees. Both of them were older, and she didn't need Wanda or Daniel getting hurt.

Millie could take care of herself.

She walked back to the shop with her copy of the quest. Art had taken the original for evidence, but she'd asked for a copy. "Just to help me think if I might have anything else to offer," she'd told him, but the truth was, therewas something about the handwriting. It kept niggling at her brain, making her wonder if maybe, just maybe, she ought to do a memory spell or something.

"Millie, wait up!"

She stopped and glanced behind her to where Lance was racing after her, panting heavily. He brushed dark hair back from his face when he finally reached her. "You walk way too fast," he said, still gulping in air.

"Says the firefighter," Millie countered. "You should be in better shape."

"I *am* in better shape. You're the one who disappeared like magic while I was talking to Art."

"Did he tell you anything else?"

Lance shook his head. "Just to wait and see if I'd be contacted again. I doubt it. I wasn't exactly contacted the first time."

That had been something she'd been curious about, too. "How *did* you get the parchment, anyway?" she asked.

She got a snort in response. "The damn thing was rolled up with a ribbon and in my locker at the station. Which, by the way, I keep locked. I figured it was one of the guys who knew my combination or something, but no one knew where it'd come from."

And Millie would bet good money that there wouldn't be any sort of video footage of the person leaving it, either. Not if they could get through locks like a professional sorcerer.

It hit her then, in a flash, just who had left the notes. "Celandine," she cursed. "I need to see if my car still starts."

"What is celandine? And why doesn't your car start? Where are you going?"

"Celandine is an irritating plant that can be toxic in some instances but therapeutic in others," she said, marching faster down the road. "My car needs a new battery, but I've been limping by with my bicycle and the bus. And I need to get to the fairgrounds." Of course, he'd be involved, the self-righteous toad. She should've seen it before, but it had been so long since she'd seen his handwriting.

Lance walked faster to keep up with her. "You know who sent the note," he said. It wasn't a question.

"I'm fairly certain I do, yes. But I can tell you that he didn't take Elizabeth." No, just needed someone else involved, and instead of calling Millie, he'd taken to older methods. Honestly, the man had to have a *phone* after all these years.

"Okay, wait," Lance said, and he jogged in front of her, bringing her to a stop. Millie's eyes narrowed, but Lance held firm. "You know he didn't do it. You're sure of this."

"It's not his style," she said, impatient now. "Move already."

"You're going the wrong way to my truck."

25 Servings of SOOP

She glared at him, bewildered. "What about your truck?"

"It doesn't have a battery problem," he said and raised an eyebrow at her. "And it's two blocks over at the station."

Oh no. "Thank you, but I'll manage," she said. When Lance didn't budge, her hands twisted into fists. "Move, Lance."

"I'm not about to leave you alone with some nutcase who's sending out messages instead of calling the police with an anonymous tip," he said firmly. "I wouldn't forgive myself if you went and wound up hurt or something, especially when I could've helped. There's already a young woman missing. Just … let me at least drive and play witness."

It wasn't the worst of requests, and Millie had to admit that he was as wrapped up in this as she was now. She wasn't thrilled with the idea of having someone non-magical along, but time was probably of the essence at this point.

"All right," she said, and Lance visibly relaxed. "But we need to swing by my shop first if just to tell Wanda that I'm going to be gone for a lot longer than I thought." And to grab a few things from her back-back office, the one no one except her, knew about. She would need to barter with Merle to get anything, and she had a feeling it was going to cost her something valuable, like the last of her dragon scales. Or maybe her harpy teeth.

After he'd had the nerve to send various knights to her shop, too.

She scowled all the way to Lance's truck. Lance, thankfully, didn't ask why.

*   *   *

The faire wasn't open to the general public until the weekend, four days away, making navigating it easy and challenging. Easy because there weren't hordes of people gathered to drink mead and watch jousts, but difficult in that they were also part of the general public, which meant they weren't supposed to be there either. They managed to get inside the main gates, step over the huge swath of mint spilling out everywhere, and toward the shops when someone called for them to stop. A young man hurried up to them, half-dressed in apparel fit for a nobleman. "The faire's not open," he said. "I'm sorry, you'll have to leave."

"I'm a vendor's friend," she said. "We're dropping off merchandise for Merlin. Please don't make us late."

The young man frowned, but his next words were what surprised her. "He's not here. He left over a week ago. I haven't seen him back since."

"He's *gone?*"

"Sorry," the young man said with a shrug. "You can drop things there for him if you want."

Merle had to have known that she would know who had sent the notes. He *had* to. "Thanks, I will," she said and headed for his shop.

Lance stayed with her; his eyes wide. "Merlin? You know a guy named Merlin?"

"His actual name is Merle," she explained. It was now, at any rate. "But Merlin sells trinkets better."

The shopfront hadn't changed in years, broken-down boards still just as broken as they had been in years prior. She was fairly certain that Merle had magicked them to do that, which made no sense to her. Why not just magic them to look clean and tidy and presentable?

The shop door was closed, but the envelope on the front made her look closer. *For Mildred* it said, and yes, he'd known she'd come. "Infuriating toad," she muttered. She wasn't at all surprised by the key and let herself in.

Lance began to follow, reminding her that she had a civilian on her hands. "Wait here," she told him. "Let me make sure he didn't leave anything behind, and then we'll go."

"You sure it's safe in there?"

"With Merle? Never, but I'm all right." She gave him a quick grin and darted in.

The inside was surprisingly tidy, given the outside, but she didn't care about the jewelry or the crystal chimes or anything near the front. No, her eyes were on the bowl set off near a wooden owl, Merlin's mark. It was more than a sign; it was a directive.

She made her way to the bowl and glanced quickly over the contents. Madder root powder, iron shavings that were bound to have come from a key, ground thulite crystals, purple candle. And a light blue satin glove with blood near the elbow.

Elizabeth's. This had to be a tracking spell.

Millie gritted her teeth. "Why didn't *you* just do it, you old nut?" she muttered under her breath. She glanced briefly behind her, but Lance was still outside, glancing around. Good. She could do this quickly and keep moving.

She mixed the ingredients and lit the candle, dropping wax on the edges to protect what was inside. Her hand reached over the bowl slowly, and she could feel the magic burning through her, rising up like a gust of air. For as long as it'd been since her last real use of magic, she'd expected more difficulty than this. Then again, her magic had always been easy to use.

With a slow exhale, she gave the magic one final push and let it out into the open.

It flowed from her fingertips, golden sparks dancing, spinning so fast that the wind sent her hair flying behind her. It pulsed with every beat of her heart, and she couldn't help the smile. It felt so *good* to let it loose, to feel it free and a part of the world again. Her oldest friend, keeping her company over the centuries. The world had moved on and abandoned her, but never the magic.

Then she felt it: cold, frightened, restrained, locked in. The old boards were harder than they looked, but they wouldn't let her out, and through the crack in the floor, a hint of mint.

The vision faded, but Millie didn't need it anymore. She knew where Elizabeth was, and it wasn't going to take but another few minutes. They could have her home by dinner.

She spun on her heel and hurried out.

"What happened?" Lance asked immediately.

"I know where she is," Millie told him. If she'd been so close, why hadn't Merle just gotten her out himself? Why leave her to her fate for over a week?

"Wait, what?"

She reached the front gates and closed her eyes. The scent of mint was almost overpowering now, and her eyes darted to the gates themselves. They were attached to thick walls, each one spanning up to a turret, wood aged but sturdy.

A gap on one side caught her attention. Something shifted in it, a flash of color, and right around the gap was a huge vine of mint.

"There," Millie said, eyes falling to the door at the base of the gate. Lance didn't hesitate, Lance didn't even ask, just pulled at the door. When it didn't budge, he backed away, then leveled his shoulder at the door.

The door swung in. Lance stumbled in after it, and Millie saw the sudden swarm of darkness bearing down on him. He began to choke, stumbling to the floor, clutching at his neck.

"No!" she shouted, racing forward, and she threw her hand out without thinking. Light magic met dark and sent the darkness flying backward, wailing as it burned to nothing.

Lance coughed and coughed but then dragged in a long breath of air. She should've known there'd be a trap, there was *always* a trap. "Are you all right?" she asked. "Lance?"

A muffled sound caught her attention. In the dark gloom, it was still easy to see Elizabeth's golden blonde hair and tear-streaked face. "Elle," Millie called, and Elizabeth's eyes flooded with fresh tears, rolling over the cloth gag. Her arm had a long scratch on it, one that was sure to match the glove Merle had left.

But she was alive and safe, frantically trying to get out of the ropes. "Hold on," Millie said, hurrying over. She couldn't use magic again, not right in front of Elizabeth, but she didn't have her pocket knife on her, either. Lance had to have something.

Elizabeth's eyes suddenly went wide in fear, and she screamed through the gag. Millie turned, a moment too late, and saw the massive shadow of a man looming over her. His eyes burned red and bright in the darkness, and his clawed hand shot toward her.

A flash of light was all Millie saw before Lance barreled into him, tackling the man to the ground. The man howled under Lance but couldn't get free, pinned by the firefighter's weight. "Go!" Lance shouted, grunting. "Get her out of here and call for help!"

Millie didn't bother trying to undo the ropes; she simply grabbed Elizabeth by the wrists and pulled. A moment later, they were outside with fresh air and sunshine.

The instant they came out, a small crowd of period-dressed people met them. Millie immediately pointed at the young man they'd met earlier. "You, call 9-1-1," she ordered to his wide and pale face. "Tell them that we've found Elizabeth Merrano, and we need backup, *now.*"

Her voice echoed without her permission, rumbling with power, and the young man pulled his cell phone out and began dialing. "Get her untied," Millie said to two nearby women, and without waiting, she darted back inside.

She heard Lance first, then the angry growl of something that was decidedly *not* human. Hell spirit? A demon? She didn't know, and she didn't have time to deal with it. The fact that Lance had kept it pinned for so long was beyond remarkable.

There was a gasp of pain that was very human, then a choking sound and Millie's heart jumped in her throat. In an instant, she threw her hand up toward the ceiling and poured every inch of her magic into the room.

The golden sparks weren't just sparks, they were flaming bolts of light, and the entire room lit up. There was an unearthly howl, loud enough to make Millie's ears ache, and then an instant later, it was gone. Slowly her magic faded out and let her see.

On the ground, unconscious, was a man with pale skin and rumpled hair. His chest rose and fell, the only sign of life she could see. He wasn't familiar to her, but he was human. That much she could see.

But it was the man beside him that caught her attention because Lance was *not* unconscious. Lance was holding his neck, small rivulets of blood rolling down to his chest, and his eyes were locked on her, wide and stunned.

Outside, the sound of sirens cut through, getting louder and louder.

"Belladonna," she swore.

*　　*　　*

Lights flashed, filling the sky with blue and red. There were police everywhere, interviewing everyone. Elizabeth sat safely in the ambulance with her mother, both smiling, which was the bright spot in it all. She'd be all right.

Art himself had come down to aid in the arrest of the man that Lance had tackled. "Three counts of assault on his record," he'd told Millie. "We've been looking for him for a while. It's a damn good thing that you two heard her when you passed by."

Millie was just glad that he'd bought their story, that they'd stumbled on Elizabeth after hearing her cries, but even more grateful that Lance had followed after without hesitation. No discrepancies, no calling her out. Nothing except following the story she'd come up with as he'd been tended to by a paramedic.

Loyal, brave, fearless, caring. All admirable traits for a knight. Merle's missive hadn't gone awry, that was for sure.

When they were finally released, Millie opted to catch a ride back with Art. He dropped her at her shop and told her that he was available to listen if she needed anything in the upcoming days. "It's never as sexy as the movies make it sound, finding a victim," he told her. "My phone line's always open for you."

Though Wanda had a million questions thanks to the gossip mill already spreading the story, Millie didn't tell her much more. All she wanted was a fresh cup of tea and to pretend that she hadn't done her magic in front of someone for the first time in hundreds of years. While she'd appreciated Lance's silence at the time, it left her unsettled now. And there was nothing she could do about it.

She was closing the counter up when the door opened. "Closing in ten," she called, pulling the last slice of banana bread out.

"Good."

Her eyes went up to where Lance stood. For a moment, they stared at each other, silence hanging between them. When Lance shoved his hands in his pockets and slowly made his way in front of the counter, Millie felt her heart began to pound. Almost five hundred years since the last time she'd been found out, and she could still feel the heat of their torches, see the glint of the pitchforks in the night.

"So."

Millie closed the glass case and refused to let her fear get the better of her. "So," she countered.

"Why do you curse in herbs?"

Millie blinked. "What?"

"You curse in herbs," he said, and his lips turned up at the corners. "It's hilarious, and I couldn't figure out what you were doing for the longest time. So why?"

Slowly she took a breath. She wasn't going to lie about any of it now. "If I curse in the usual terms, it tends to … end up hexing someone. So, I just stopped."

Unbelievably, his lips turned up even more. This wasn't going anywhere close to how she'd expected it to go. "You know I'm a witch," she said. It wasn't a question.

Lance raised both eyebrows. "I know what I saw in that room. The first time, when something started choking me, I thought I'd just been seeing things. Then you came back and lit up the room like a fireworks stand going off."

"You followed my lead when we told Art what had happened," she said, bewildered. "Why would you do that when you knew what I was?"

"Because you saved my life." It was said matter-of-factly like it was the weather. "You had my back like anyone at the station would have. Whatever I was fighting wasn't the man that wound up in the back of the cop car. It was something more. It's gone now, right?"

Millie tried to find her voice in the wake of his explanation. "Yeah. It's not coming back." Not after what she'd done.

He shrugged. "Then we're good. Except for one thing."

And her heart had just started beating at normal speeds, too. "Yes?"

His eyes danced. "I never got my orange scones from this morning. I was too busy setting off on a quest. And I'm pretty sure I was promised a bounty."

Technically, Merle had promised the bounty. Whatever the old wizard had involved himself in would probably circle back around to her at some point. And, unfortunately for Lance, it would most likely drag him along too. Knights were easy to come by. Knights who had completed quests were a far rarer commodity.

Knights with a witch for a questing partner? Very rare indeed.

She grabbed two scones and the last slice of banana bread. "Your bounty, good sir knight," she told him.

135

"And a good day to you, fair witch," he said, giving her a deep bow. He left then with a wave and the paper bag in his hand.

Slowly Millie began to grin. A moment later, she threw her hand toward the door, locking it behind him.

A good day indeed.

∾

J.M. Rhineheart is a speculative fiction writer working on her first full-length novel. She has been published in several anthologies, including "The Devil You Know" and "Rowan & Oak". If she's not writing, she's visiting national parks to see new sights and running races to earn some sweet swag. She lives in Virginia with her family, and she teaches music and English.

BIRD ON A WIRE
KAITLYN TOVADO

"You're doing well."

I bristle at the use of the word "well".

Psychologists—more commonly referred to by the rest of the public as psychotherapists—should avoid using words that express a sense of negative versus positive. It conveys to their patients—more commonly referred to by the general public as psychotics—that there is an expectation of controlling your symptoms. Psychotherapy is becoming a dying job as the government discovers more and more "cures" for mental illnesses. They were tired of the ten-year process of a doctor slowly pulling your brain apart like a piece of string to find the knot somewhere deep in your psyche.

No, they wanted something quick. Here's a pill, an injection, a treatment—that will fix it. They had drugs long before the government went all Big Brother-esque, but I've always been told that you took hundreds of them over your lifetime, constantly switching until they found the "right mix." It was dangerous mixing all those pills together, and the health risks started to outweigh the benefits. So, now they have one quick fix, and it's done. Still, I've always been a special case. Every time I wind up back in the doctor's office curled in on myself like a piece of burning paper, they always sigh, shooting the cure into my arm again. Their agitation is palpable, as they can't understand why I can't be fixed like everyone else. So, they sent me here, to the psychotherapist, where only the truly fucked up cases go. It has become a trendy topic at school as the whisper of "Psycho, psycho, psycho" passes from mouth to mouth. I am a relic of a life long since passed.

Simply based on the ambiance of my psychotherapist's office, I know that my therapist has long since been out of practice. She requires that you bring your own tissues because she can't afford to provide them herself. Just to piss her off, I bought a pack of tissues from a street vendor. It has a picture of a nun waving a handkerchief with the words *Bless You* in tie-dye below it. I see her eyes narrow every time I pull one out, and it seems like a massive middle finger to her.

Her usual dime store artworks of flowers have been replaced by dark surrealist paintings. Mozart's *Requiem* is always blasting through the speakers on repeat, which I feel is a truly inappropriate song to be playing in an office for the mentally ill, but no one really asked me. The windows are covered in heavy drapes, and I laughingly asked her at the beginning of one session if she was a vampire. She narrowed her eyes and asked me if that was really what I wanted to talk about. I noticed that she didn't answer the question. It doesn't matter. Even if vampires really existed, the government would probably have a cure for that too.

"Well enough," I reply, looking out the window. I'm holding my breath, as if staying as still as possible will keep her from saying what she's about to say. If I don't move, maybe she won't be able to nail me to the wall. I knew it would happen eventually. The government is unwilling to return to a time before cures and leave me to get better on my own. They give me a shot of the DPRSN/ANXTY/B-PLR cure every month, and it keeps my symptoms at bay. I'm less likely to shrink back at school when someone calls me a psycho than to grab them by the collar and slam them up against the wall. This reaction is apparently more acceptable.

"I think it's about time you get the procedure. You're several years behind most of your classmates."

There. Like an arrow, the words pierce through my heart. I don't want the procedure; perhaps I even stayed this sick simply to avoid it.

"I don't have a choice, do I?"

I'm still staring out the window, but my breath unhitches. It doesn't matter if she sees me now because the threat has already been thrown out there. The light filtering through the window, stirring up the dust, barely penetrates the darkness in her office.

25 Servings of SOOP

"No, you do not have a choice. If you do not get the procedure done while you are in a current state of normality, I will be forced to stop seeing you, and your monthly dose of the cure will be cut off. If that does happen, we predict that you will kill yourself within two months, three at the most. Then you will no longer be a burden on the state. The last time we talked of suicide, you said if you were going to do it, you would hang yourself. Suppose you refuse to get the procedure, which is your right as a mental patient. In that case, we will provide you with the rope, which may move our projection up a bit and will remove your drain on scarce public resources."

She says it in a matter-of-fact fashion with her attention fixated on the giant spring that she's passing from hand to hand. A toy from before my parents' time, its name started with an "s", I think. Her words are callous but devoid of emotion, which makes it better. She's not saying these words maliciously as there is no anger. This is what she is required to say by the government, straight to the point, matter-of-fact.

"Well, I suppose I should get it done then," I add, watching her twist and untwist the toy in her lap,

"I believe that would be wise. You can set it up with my secretary."

The procedure is simple to understand if you're a doctor. If you're tall, they place wires through all of your limbs that connect in the middle of your chest to a giant crank. If you're short, they use spacers. It either stretches your limbs or constricts them 'til you're the appropriate 5'8" tall, which is the designated height of every citizen of the World Organization. Apparently, sometime in the mid-2000s, scientists stumbled upon irrefutable evidence that revealed that equality and world peace could be reached by creating a height restriction. It had been proven that taller political candidates consistently won in every single poll, and there was no such thing as a short supermodel, or one who looked like Sasquatch once you put her into 4-inch heels.

It made so much sense. I'm sure there was more evidence than that. Still, the history books are a little sketchy on the details, which leaves the door wide open for conspiracy theories. Things like the government can control you through the wires, forcing your limbs to move against your will, and while you're under, they mess with your brain—all sorts of fun possibilities. It didn't

Bird on a Wire Kaitlyn Tovado

really matter. If you wanted to be a citizen, which means living in a safe neighborhood, provided with a food and water allowance, and the ability to vote, you had to have it done. Psychotics like me were allowed to put it off for a few years, because the scientists had realized that the excruciating pain endured during the procedure time could drive normal people to madness but it drove the mentally ill into complete hysteria. But now that I'm "stable," —oh how I loathe that word—it seems it's my time now.

I open my eyes, and my vision is blurry. I fight to keep them open, but I'm not able to. They close against my will, and I drift into that twilight area of sleep where you're aware of the world around you but not capable of participating in it. I can hear voices, and the back of my eyelids burn red as bright light filters through them. On some level, I can tell that the voices are talking about me and the words are not positive, but I'm so tired. I can't seem to bring myself to care. I doze for a while until my eyes open again. At first, I'm confused, unsure where I am or why I'm tied down to a bed. I let out a blood-curdling scream, and a face appears above me while a hand firmly covers my mouth.

"It's okay. You're in the hospital. You're fine, but I really can't have you screaming as you'll scare the other patients." Slowly, the words filter through my groggy mind, and I nod, letting the nurse know that I understand what she's saying. She removes her hand and smiles down at me.

"Well, everything went fine. No runs. No hits. No errors." She giggles, like this is some kind of joke I should be in on. "Now, you need to remain calm. You're going to feel the wires moving under your skin, but after a while, you won't even notice it. But I really don't want you freaking out when you see the crank. It always seems to freak people out, though I don't know why. I can cover your mouth again if you want."

She smiles down at me, expecting an answer. I shake my head, not willing to form words yet. She undoes the straps holding me down to the bed, explaining they're to keep me from rolling out while I'm asleep.

At first, I don't move at all. I want to not feel those wires with every fiber of my being, but eventually, the nurse lets out an impatient huff. Slowly, I begin to sit up, and I cringe at the sensation of wires crawling under my skin. I lift my shaking hand an inch at a time to grasp the hem of the blanket that's covering my chest.

"Please don't scream," the nurse adds again, and I can feel myself murmur a consenting yes. I contemplate pulling the blanket down a little at a time but decide it's better to rip it off like a band-aid. With a grand flourish, I throw the blanket back and gape down at my chest. A large silver gear—like something out of a Steampunk novel—glows brightly, placed dead center in the middle of my chest, taking up almost all of the space between my breasts.

I am unable to keep my promise.

I scream.

∽

Kat Tovado has been writing stories since the fourth grade. In high school, she was selected as one of two freshmen to attend the prestigious arts and humanities program in her city. She graduated with an AA in English with an emphasis in creative writing and was one out of twenty-five writers awarded the Air Force Club Member Scholarship for her essay in a nationwide contest. She lives in Colorado Springs and is currently working on her debut novel. You can find her on Instagram @kat.tovado.author, on Twitter @kattovadoauthor, or her Facebook page @kattovadoauthor

DOORS BETWEEN
JUSTIN ATTAS

Click—just sparks, no flame from the silver lighter.

"Damn this thing." El's frame shook as her teeth mashed the cigarette between her lips. Out of fluid at a time like this. The chilled wind seized her hair and long brown coat and whipped them around like broken playthings. She crossed her arms over the tasteful amount of cleavage unprotected by her collared shirt.

The whole of Doorhinge was laid out before her. It was a fantastic viewpoint, as she had been assured. With a name like Doorhinge, Eleanor had come to town with an expectation of oddity, but nothing like what she had seen. She let out a long, misty breath while she gripped the picture in her pocket.

"I'm sorry, Sal," she said to the girl in the photograph. "You know this is a crock, right?" She knew her friend would nod her head if she could. But still, she was not ready to leave just yet. El's occupation came with a certain degree of insatiable curiosity. She knew it was a bad call, but one she had to make.

"If you're not back in a week, I'll come to get you myself." Even her easy-going husband, Rich, half-joked before she left. She exchanged the picture for her dilapidated notebook and a stubby pencil. Her ice-blue eyes swam through her crammed detective scribbles.

"Sure, the people are a little off, but it's nice enough," a first-year resident of Doorhinge, not yet fully assimilated into local culture, had said. "Your friend isn't the first disappearance we've had. The police just can't seem to figure it out." These were the same police that so cordially opened up their records to El.

142

When Sally Mallord had reappeared, she had been dismembered at every major joint and several minor ones.

"If you're looking to learn the layout of the town, head up to Osprey Ridge," the resident had told her at the end of their conversation. And there El was.

How the local law hadn't found anything she couldn't fathom—until she saw for herself. There was no sign of struggle. There was no weapon, not even a trail of blood. The amount that Sal bled, there should have been clear footprints painted to the door. It was as if she had just fallen apart. El gagged a little and pounded a fist to her chest. In all her years on the force, that had hardly ever happened. She scanned further down the page. "A little off" didn't even begin to describe Doorhinge's other residents.

"Sometimes he has to cut us up," the butcher had said. El asked who. "The Fisherman." That was all she could get out of the woman before she became entranced, cleaving raw hunks of steak into bloody bits (*Completely despondent*, El had scrawled there).

"He thins the flock," the tailor with a lazy eye had droned. "We're all in the chain, all on his list. Everyone knows someone." He told El, "The Fisherman," when asked. At this point, El began questioning directly about the Fisherman.

One wayward woman hummed the entire time El tried to speak to her.

"If the doorway's cracked, turn right back," the only child she could find chimed.

After that came the barely legible scratches. These people had rattled along too quickly to neatly record.

"Keep dangling bait, see what bites," then, "Or maybe you're the one chasing the hook." Another said, "His song is always different, depending on the audience." (Noted along with the humming woman). "Once you're in his waters, nobody can help you," by a fourteen-year-old. By far the strangest, though, was the mortician. His exchange was written in particularly poor penmanship due to El's resultant shaking.

"Take this," Gary the mortician had offered her Sal's severed, stark-white finger, "Some people think if you keep a part of the bait, he can't get you." At this point, El had shuffled uncomfortably away, but he moved closer. By the look of his post-mortem work, Gary was skilled, yet seemed subject to the same strange behavior as everyone else in town.

She flipped the page and turned her eyes over the town of Doorhinge. Her pencil swirled and sliced in elegant motions while her eyes darted across the town. She outlined the locations of the General Store, the East Coast Bank, St. Anthony's Parish, Andrew's Fish Market, Fert's Dress, and Marien's Meats.

"Maybe Andrew can tell me a little more about it." El circled his place on her hand-scrawled map. It was rather well done for what little time she had spent on it. She snapped her notebook closed and dropped it in her coat.

The trail back to town was much easier on the way down than up, with its jagged rocky steps pointed away. El prided herself mostly on her analytical skills, but she was no pushover and bounded down the path with ease. The trailhead was dry and dead as the ridge, comprised of dead grey grass and skeletal trees. From here, she followed the sidewalk down Main Street and turned onto Crowley. She went four buildings down to Andrew's Fish Market. It was half-past six, and the sun had retreated behind overcast clouds hours ago. She hadn't seen anyone on her way. The "open" sign was hung, so she tapped the door's glass a few times. No one came to meet her.

"Hello?" El knocked harder, and the door creaked half open with a wail that made her cringe. The peg that normally would have kept it closed was broken. She could see through the opening that someone was inside, staring at her. There was a glow around the figure, maybe an old-style oil lantern, which obscured its features. The door swung closed. The light flickered out.

"Excuse me?" El pushed her way through without invitation. The place was empty—no customers, no salesperson. It was much warmer than outside, which she thought a bit odd. She dissected several aisles of glass cases. Inside, fish laid on ice. With her husband being a fisherman, El knew this was an impressive catch.

"Hello?" Something rustled in a backroom behind the check-out counter. "I just have a few questions."

The light went on again behind a magazine rack. El rounded a fish case after it, but the bearer bolted away. Fleeing footsteps echoed as if through an amphitheater.

25 Servings of SOOP

"Please," El raced past the rack, but the runner was gone.

She strafed after the light and sound between several snack stands in her uncomfortable new flats. She flew with it right down a dark, slender hallway. The light vanished behind a closing door at the end of the hall labeled "restroom". El rushed past an office on the left and slammed into the restroom door, which swung in freely. Inside, she gasped so hard it brought on a fit of coughs.

"Sal?" There was no mistaking that blazing yellow hair and green marble eyes. Her expression was flat, but her lips quivered like she was trying to say something. "No—this can't…" El muttered. But it was Sal. Her skin shimmered like a lighthouse beacon. Her attempts to speak continued in a sputter of gurgles. El cleared her throat in honor of her friend's memory, little as she believed in this sort of thing. "Wh-what is it?" she said. Sal's arm twitched up abruptly to reach for her friend.

"El."

The next instant, Sal's skin peeled away into flower petals of skin, blood, and bone. They scattered and smoldered into dust around a filth-smeared mirror. Sal left El only a dirty reflection of herself to stare at.

"I need to get out of here." El jammed her hands in her pockets and grabbed a cigarette and her lighter. Maybe there was a drop of lighter fluid left somewhere in there.

She about-faced as she snapped the striker back several times with her thumb. Nothing, not even a spark. She let out a heavy breath of laughter at how ridiculous she was being. She had not let herself mourn Sal, really, and she had been under a lot of stress chasing her phantom killer. Hallucinations were not out of the question. However, her chuckles ceased when she noticed she could see her breath as clearly as if she had taken a draw from her cigarette.

"I need to get out of here," she reaffirmed, and she shoved through the door.

A face peeked out of the darkness and almost collided with hers. El lunged back, and her breath was sharp and sporadic as she stared into the grizzled, grey visage. It was colorless as the trees on Osprey Ridge.

"H-hello," she tried to pull herself together. The man looked right through her. "Are you Andrew?" He merely mumbled something and reached for a black garbage bag El just noticed.

"Won't be gettin' me," the presumed Andrew murmured. El looked on silently as he shouldered the bumpy sack and turned away. After a few calming breaths, she followed him back through the fish-cases to the front door. Here he dumped the bag, which popped open. It puffed out a breath of odor so rancid that El trapped her vomit mid-throat with a clutching hand to avoid a scene. "Watch over me, Danny," Andrew grunted.

He reached down into the bag and pulled up a red-stained cord, dangling like a vein. On a closer look, El saw the twisted barbs. Her hand flew from her throat to her mouth when he hauled a pale, dried arm from the sack. She fought urges to scream as Andrew pulled up an entire body's worth of parts—legs, hands, ears, and other various chunks of severed flesh. His human-on-a-string hung over the door on pegs in a perfect arch like a set of Christmas lights. The very second Andrew stepped away from the door, El burst through and sprinted down Crowley Street.

"What the hell?" she spat through gasps. "What the hell?"

"El," simple, crisp, innocent. There was no doubting it was Sal's voice, but El kept running. "El," it repeated, eerily warm, like a mother waking her child, "El," but she didn't stop. She was heading for the town's outskirts, for her car. Then the only thing in the world that could slow her down happened—her best friend of fifteen years materialized, ethereal light and all, right in front of her.

"Sal!" El's shoes scraped against the withered old pavement.

"El," the image said. Liquid rubies cascaded down Sal's trembling lips and chin. A piece of metal poked through her neck and curved back—a hook. A thin wire stretched taut from her throat back to someone hidden in her shadow. Even under such duress, El's mind rotated the pieces of this contorted puzzle until they finally fit into place. Her notes rang through her head like a warped church bell.

Some people think if you keep a part of the bait, he can't get you—Andrew's string.

His song is always different, depending on the audience. For her, it was Sal.

If the doorways crack, turn right back—the entrance to the fish market.

Once you're in his waters, no one can help you. The way Andrew looked right through her.

Like a loosed arrow, a metal triangle slid through El's spine, out the front of her neck. Scarlet mist sprayed onto the pavement as she reached instinctively for the site of the wound. Her lips quaked when she tried to talk.

"Rich," she gurgled and tried again, "Rich." It was all she could say. She and Sal were trapped, staring at one another for a while before a tug on both their lines pulled them away.

We're all in a chain, all on his list.

El caught sight of her own body laid out on the ground, her parts splayed in scarlet across the pavement.

"Rich," she said again as she was being yanked away into the bait bucket.

Everyone knows someone.

∾

Justin Attas is a published author, professional ghostwriter, licensed teacher, and writing mentor. He has written twelve novels across various genres—western, supernatural, mystery, crime thriller, and others. Justin is also the author of the science fiction novel, Strand: The Silver Radio. *He has a background in education, which he uses to create articles and videos to help other writers along their journeys. As someone who had a crooked journey to writing, Justin aspires to use his experience and skills to encourage anyone with the soul of a writer to "grab a pen" and start writing.*

REUBEN

REGAN W. H. MACAULAY

"Clarissa, he's an abomination," said Father Simmons, stifling a dry cough.

"Now, Father, you promised me no melodramatic piety," Clarissa said in a strained voice, feeling a flush of heat in her cheeks. Her jaw stiffened as she held her newborn close. "I think the term 'abomination' qualifies as melodramatic."

Now, it was Father Simmons's turn to go red in the face. He rose from his seat, his lips tense and white. "This is serious, Clarissa," the Father hissed, his eyes sharp as pins. "You should not have made him."

"Made him," she repeated with a rasp in her throat. Clarissa averted her gaze.

"What else would you call it?" Simmons retorted. "Heed me now; they will come for young Reuben. They'll take him from you, and they will destroy him."

Clarissa pulled baby Reuben so close she could have smothered him. She wished she could swallow him and hide him from the world and this rabid priest. Father Simmons relinquished his scrutiny, turned from Clarissa and the baby, and walked out the front door. Clarissa shot up from her seat, Reuben still pinned to her chest, and bolted the door shut behind the priest. She returned with baby Reuben to the chaise and stared into nothingness. The whole world wanted to steal her happiness.

*   *   *

A man—more bandages, blood, and bruises than clean flesh—lay before her wrapped in white sheets. One eye was swollen shut. The other was staring at her, filled with tears and regret. He cannot speak to her, but she knows he doesn't want to leave her. But he will leave. And they will miss so much time together. She feels the immediacy of a throb lodged in her throat—the pain radiates throughout her body, mind, and soul. She will have someone to care for again and someone to take care of her someday. No one and nothing will rob her of the right all loving couples have to be together always.

*   *   *

Reuben's fussing awoke her from her paranoid reverie, and she cradled his head while fishing her breast out from her buttoned-up blouse. She offered her nipple to the infant, and he accepted it greedily. She watched him feed and fell in love with him all over again.

"You are mine, and I am yours," she cooed to him as he suckled. "I will raise you to be a man, and you will protect me when I am old and frail. That's our bargain."

Reuben's gums released her areola. Clarissa watched him fade into a contented sleep. "No one is taking you away from me," she whispered.

Gently rising to her feet, she carried her baby to his crib, which was stationed in the living room so she could constantly keep an eye on him. She laid him on his stomach and hovered over him a while before turning away with a sigh. Her landline handset blinked at her. It held messages she longed to avoid. More preachy nonsense from friends and family professing to care, but none of them understood. Clarissa walked over to the handset and picked it up slowly. She held it to her ear, played back the message, and exhaled.

"Clarissa, it's your mother. Again. Please pick up the phone, honey. I need to talk to you. Your husband is gone, Clarissa, gone almost a year now. You have to move on—"

Clarissa paused the message and erased it. Next message: "Clarissa, it's Trudy. Call me when you can, okay? Bye," and beep. Erase. Next message, a click and dial tone. End of messages.

She hung up and stared at the phone in her hand. When it rang, she jumped. She checked Reuben, but the ring hadn't woken him. She pressed the answer button. "Hello?"

"Hey, Claire, it's me," a perky voice replied—Trudy calling back. "How are you?"

"Get to the point, Trude," Clarissa sighed.

"Right to the point, eh?" Trudy said, still sounding chipper. A pause of awkward silence passed.

"It's okay, Trude. I've heard it all these past few days since bringing Reuben home from the hospital. Lay it on me." Another sigh.

"I hear scary things from people, Claire. I'm afraid for you. You shouldn't have done it."

"Shouldn't have had Reuben, you mean."

"Yes."

"I deserve him, goddamnit! I love him!"

"I know, Claire, I know. It's just so weird. People are not going to accept this. By making him, you've put him and yourself in danger."

"'By making him—you make it sound like I put him together in a lab."

"Well, how did you do it? He's a clone, right?"

"Yes, but I was still the surrogate."

"That doesn't make it any better. You're his mother and his wife?"

"Yes!" Tears gathered in Clarissa's eyes—her voice grew hoarse again.

"People think that's sick."

Clarissa sobbed. "It's not sick; he's my…"

"Your what? Your son? Your husband? So long as you have someone to look after you eventually, right?"

"You don't understand! You have your husband. You have your children. You weren't left alone!" Clarissa wiped her eyes roughly. Reuben stirred in the crib.

"I do understand, but Reuben is dead. You move on—that's all you can do! You don't do this. You don't recreate and raise your own husband's double. It's just all kinds of wrong."

Clarissa covered her eyes with her hand. She crumbled to the floor and tried to catch her breath.

25 Servings of SOOP

"I don't know, maybe you should think about leaving. Or give him up."
Clarissa's mind drifted back to the hospital one year ago…

* * *

The morgue in the hospital's basement had aqua-colored walls and was lit dimly
by several fluorescent fixtures. Her husband was locked inside a drawer, now.

"So Humanex will do it?" Clarissa mumbled.

The mortician flinched at her whisper. "Yes. I'll send the sample to them
myself," she replied in a voice even lower than Clarissa's. "They won't ask
questions. There will be no documentation."

"And when will they…" Clarissa swallowed, but no other words would
leave her lips.

"I will contact you in a few weeks," the mortician, her old high school
friend, replied. "They will inseminate you on site."

* * *

"I will not give him up!" Clarissa screamed into the phone. Reuben shrieked.
Clarissa hung up the phone and threw it across the room. She scrambled to her
feet and rushed over to the crib. Tears and mascara streaked down her face as
she lifted little Reuben out of the crib and held him in her arms.

"We'll leave. That's what we'll do," she sobbed to the baby in her arms.
"We'll go where no one knows who you are. You are mine, and I am yours.
I will raise you to be a man, and you will protect me when I am old and frail.
That's our bargain."

*Regan W. H. Macaulay is an award-winning author of novels, short stories, children's
literature, and scripts. Writing is her passion, but she's also a producer and director
of theatre, film, and television. She is an animal enthusiast as well, which led her
to become a certified canine and feline massage therapist. She is the author of* The

Trilogy of Horrifically Half-baked Ham, *which includes "Space Zombies!" (based on her film, "Space Zombies: 13 Months of Brain-Spinning Mayhem!" available on iTunes and DVD), "They Suck", and "Horror at Terror Creek". Coming soon, Regan's first middle-grade novel series,* Peter Little Wing.

THE WILL
KRISTALYN A. VETOVICH

God has a plan for all of us. Is that not what they say?

I was certainly not of that opinion when the book found its way to me.

I was young. Too young to understand much of the world, but old enough to know that there was no God in the Great War, at least none that I could see.

Between 1914 and 1918, the war had come to Hooge too many times for me to believe that it would ever leave us, and now it had come again.

It was November in Belgium. I was thirteen, and our home had already become a memorial to what we all had thought would be the War to End All Wars.

If only, yes? The battles had taken much from my family because they had taken much of my family—cousins, grandparents, and my father earlier that same year. Having lost my mother years before to an illness, I had resigned myself when I heard the thunder return that, this time, I would follow them, not by choice, but by inevitability.

To be fair, this mentality did help to numb the fear. I was completely indifferent as I watched from the window of the church that we always took shelter in. Bullets flew, soldiers cried out to a Maker who I had not witnessed the mercy of in years, and I watched, feeling only just enough interest to continue taking in the absurdity of it all.

What was the point, these men from so many nations shooting and shouting? Half of them could not hope to know what the others were saying,

153

though I imagine the words were not so different in meaning. And all this simply because no one would be the first to say, "No more." It was the mindless plight of fools, in my opinion, and I had no respect for it.

The church priest tugged on my shoulder, telling me it was urgent that I keep away from the windows, but I disagreed. He left me to fate when my younger sister began crying.

Save the ones you still can, Father, I had thought to myself. Take care of her. This world is done with me, and I am certainly done with it.

A thunderous shot brought me to attention, and I settled my eyes to the street, where I saw a man stumbling away from the fighting. Normally, I would not have blamed the man for choosing to desert the fight, but he displayed no signs of running from anything. Instead, he seemed to be seeking something out.

And then his eyes settled on me. I nearly ducked away but remembered that I did not care if he took my life, so I remained still, looking down at him through the window.

The man squinted at me and then looked down to consult the pages of a thin book in the palm of his hand. Then he looked at me in an entirely new way.

It seemed he had found what he was looking for, and I wondered if God was real and was personally attending to my decision to forgo life.

Suddenly, I was nervous. I remembered what I had told my sister only weeks before: *if you begin something, finish it, and do it as soon as possible.* I had filled my father's shoes quickly and with little patience, so in my young mind, dragging things out only led to meaningless disaster as I had seen for most of my life.

In my final moments, I decided I would show my sister that I was no hypocrite. I climbed through the broken glass, which had once been a lovely stained-glass window. I walked toward the soldier because it was better if my death didn't endanger anyone else.

The man seemed impressed as he slowed his pace to stop in front of me. I only looked at him as he bent one knee to meet me at my height. He said things that I could not comprehend. He spoke French.

He tried to speak to me several times, but it did not take long for him to realize that I did not understand. His brows drew together as he decided on a new tactic. He moved the old book from under his arm and held it out to me.

He spoke again and pointed at it repeatedly. Now I knew that it must be important.

I looked down at the book and back to him before cautiously placing a hand on the cover.

He nodded vigorously, his eyes glinting. I recognized what I saw in them. Hope. It had been a long time since I had seen it reflected in someone's eyes. It made this book all the more intriguing.

Not yet willing to commit, I simply brushed my fingers across the cover. It was ancient and rough. Something about it reminded me of my grandfather, to be honest. The warmth of the memories made me even more willing to accept the Frenchman's gift, though I was sure I would not be able to read this book. I could not even discern the title back then. *La Volonté*. The whole book would be in French. What use was that to me?

The man saw the doubt in my eyes. He continued to push the book toward me until finally, I was startled into taking it without thinking. I was so intent on shoving it back at him that I nearly missed it.

Once the book was secure in my hands, I swear to you, the title changed. Now it read *De Wil*. The Will.

Frightened by whatever witchcraft this was, I threw the book back at the Frenchman. It hit him but fell to the ground, and he laughed. He picked it up and held it out to me. The title remained in Dutch.

He said something in a gentle tone, his eyes gleaming with kindness, though his smile was so sad.

I accepted the book this time, purely out of shock and respect for the tears collecting in the Frenchman's eyes. He reached forward, placing a hand on the book as if it were an old friend. He lifted the cover just enough to see the words inside, which must have remained in French unless he could also read Dutch. His breath caught in his throat, but he smiled anyway. The tears began to fall, and he looked at me, still smiling but breathing too quickly.

"Merci," he whispered, and his next words I will never forget. *"Dieu vous bénisse."* He took in a very deep, shuddering breath and closed his eyes, placing a steadying hand on my shoulder. *"Dieu vous bénisse…"*

Suddenly, I remembered the war. The gunshot reminded me but not quickly enough to save him. It pierced him. I never did know exactly where, but he fell onto me and was gone before he met my shoulder.

I fell backward, scrambling away from him and throwing the book in the process. He was dead. He had just died in front of me.

Not this again. It was too much for me. My vision blurred, and I barely remembered to grab the book before I ran back to the shelter of the church. The fear of battle had returned, accompanied by a curiosity that would not let me leave this world until I knew why that man had sought me out.

So, I lived, as you can plainly see, and it was not long before the sun finally began to rise on the world again. The war came to an end, and I could breathe deeply.

My sister and I were left with few options, but the priest took us into his care. It was months before I discovered why. He would not allow us to be taken or separated, and I knew that it had something to do with the look he had given me when I had returned with *De Wil*. There had been shock on his face, of course, but also recognition. I did not know how he could have heard about the book, but his eyes lingered on it with a sense of reverence. It was familiar to him.

I was suspicious of him, and he sensed it. My sister and I worked for our keep. I became acquainted with the church and its workings, even participating in Sunday services as necessary, but never happily.

I lived for the darkness. When I was allowed to return to my room at the end of the day, I would read the book by candlelight, and I saw things: names of people I would never meet and things that they needed to know or do, even how to help them. Every night the story would change. Upon opening the cover, the words would be different, telling new people and circumstances that required attention.

I could not decide what it meant or why it was mine to hold. It was not long before the priest confronted me about it.

I was too absorbed in the story to hear his footsteps. I could only close the book as quickly as possible and try to ignore his presence.

"Jansen, what are you reading?" he asked softly so as not to make me defensive.

It did not work. I was always defensive, but respect was necessary and a trait my father valued.

"Nothing of importance, Father Bediende."

"Please do not ever say that about this book, Jansen. It is so far from the truth," he said. And then I turned to look at him.

The feeling of vindication was short-lived once the questions rushed into my mind. I had to subdue my instinctual accusing tone before I could ask him what he knew about *De Wil*.

I had to surrender my resolve to shut him out. I had to lose the battle that only I fought. However, that loss would gain me everything.

"*De Wil*," Father Bediende breathed as he entered the room. "I never thought I would see it in my own language, least of all in the hands of a young man like you. Mysterious ways indeed…" His voice trailed off, and his eyes stared into the void, unseeing.

I remained impatiently silent. The only words in my mind would have been disrespectful.

"God has a plan for all of us," Father Bediende began, and before I could roll my eyes, he continued. "This is that plan, Jansen. You hold it in your hands."

The shock and confusion must have been apparent on my face. Of course, I knew that this book was beyond normal, but I had never dreamed that there was such a grand scheme behind it. The stories I had been reading were the plans of God? How was that possible?

"God gives everyone a purpose," he explained, "and some are meant to help and guide the others in order to preserve God's ultimate plan. Everyone is important and deserves the chance to make their own choices to decide their fates, so God sends them people to speak on His behalf." Then he smiled at me the way my mother used to. "I am one of those people. *De Wil* is my guide. I am connected to it. God's will is on my heart and in my mind, so I know what to do. As long as *De Wil* exists, those who are like me will have the wisdom to help people worldwide. *De Wil* is our anchor, and you are its keeper."

His words made the small book feel heavier in my hands. A voice in my head argued against Father Bediende's claim, but I wanted it to be true. I wanted the book to give me a purpose, so I kept my mind open.

"That book kept me from you these past few months," Father Bediende continued, as though complimenting Del Wil's cleverness, "and tonight it called me to you. Turn the page."

I did and immediately saw what he meant. There, on the page, was my name, and words…

"A time to speak," Father Bediende said aloud as I read. "Ecclesiastes 3:7. That was all I needed to know that it was time to explain your purpose to you."

And the lessons began. He told me of how the book connects the people who are meant to preserve God's plan.

"Many people confuse us for psychics, but there is much more to our calling than seeing the future. We see what choices need to be made, and we encourage them—never force them. God's people are not slaves."

It was overwhelming, but he promised that I would understand in time. This was not what I wanted to hear. My curiosity began a trend of several years that would see Father Bediende and myself become very close.

I spent years learning my place in the grand scheme of *De Wil*'s history—more of a legacy, really. It was passed on from one keeper to another, and I was simply the latest in a line that dated back to the day the Lord sent the Holy Ghost.

I remained reasonably skeptical of God for quite a while before finally accepting that the book's very existence had to be enough proof of His existence. He put it here as a physical link between His plan and the people meant to keep it in line. Without *De Wil*, people like Father Bediende would have no foundation and no way of knowing what God's plan is. And whether I wanted to believe these things or not, I had a job to do, and I took that very seriously. It wasn't until the worst happened that I finally surrendered myself to faith.

When I was old enough, Father Bediende and I agreed that it was best for me to move elsewhere. I would not be safe in one place for much longer.

Among those meant to help people were those who chose to manipulate them instead. The population of those with the gift to know *De Wil* could be split by very blurred lines into three factions: those who followed it, those who sought to control it, and those who wanted to destroy it, which would leave the people who could interpret its instructions helpless in their cause. The only person between the world and the book was me. I needed to hide to protect *De Wil* and ensure that only honest people came into contact with it. The best way to accomplish that was to surround myself with people. I would become the needle in the proverbial haystack.

In Brussels. Father Bediende had contacts there and many other places, thanks to the missions he had received from *De Wil*. He arranged for me to stay in Brussels and continue my work within a church there. It seemed that Father Bediende intended for me to follow in his footsteps, and I had little time to argue.

The plan to hide in Brussels was only somewhat successful. Among the many tasks that I was given to contribute to the new church and practice discipline was the gathering of supplies for the services and the members of the church. The elderly needed food, the poor needed clothing, and the church was eager to be the hands and feet of the Lord … by making use of my own.

This task held no interest for me outside of the chance to escape the confines of the old and dusty cathedral.

Knowing what I did about the book, I hated the moments when I was not learning more about it, and what that had to do with me, so I kept my excursions short.

But on one particular day, I found my path cut off by a smug-looking man, not much older than me but old enough to think me insignificant.

"So, it is you?" he asked. I did not answer. He was not pleased. He gave a shout, and two other men emerged behind him. I might have worked for the church, but I was not the type to turn the other cheek, much to Father Bediende's frustration. Clearly, these men wanted to control or to destroy *De Wil*, and I would not stand for that. I merely planted my feet and wore a challenge on my face. The book was secure in my pocket. I was a useless orphan. I meant nothing to them. The only thing that made me unique was *De Wil.* They would not lay a finger on it while I was still breathing.

I was such a stubborn child. The head of the group saw my movement and smiled at me, apparently pleased that it would come down to fighting.

I had seen and lost enough in life to make me a furious young man, and I carried that anger with me on my path to adulthood. I had used it in Hooge to defend my sister on several occasions, and I had no issues using it to protect myself now.

Without waiting for a cause, the man threw a fist toward my face, but I ducked and targeted his stomach, taking the air from him.

This was not well received by his accomplices, and they, too, set upon me, taking turns between beating me and grabbing for the book.

I had the advantage, however. The moment must have taken priority in a larger design because the words of the book filled my mind, alerting me to the best courses of action. I took them, ducking, punching, and swinging various limbs in the appropriate directions.

When it was finished, and I staggered back onto a busier street, I found my shoulders caught by a man. I nearly broke his nose until he assured me that the book had called him to guide me back to the church.

I was admonished and not allowed to appear during that Sunday's service. An altar boy with blackened eyes would not lend itself to the church's reputation, but I did not care. I welcomed the opportunity to avoid the services, and it was sure to happen again.

In fact, it became the norm whenever I was discovered by the wrong people, those who sought to oppose the instructions of *De Wil* rather than to facilitate them.

Just imagine knowing of history's most pivotal moments before they occur. For some, the taste of power is too strong a drug. These were the people whom, due to the lessons I was given in Latin, I dubbed the *Iniquus.* And those who came to me with the intent of giving people the choice to follow *De Wil* or asking my advice because they could sense that I was the book's keeper, I called the *Optio.*

I encountered them everywhere, even when I entered the Catholic University of Leuven when I was old enough.

I had developed a deep interest in history and studied it at the university. I could almost trace the path of *De Wil* through the pages of my textbooks. My enthusiasm impressed the school enough to earn me several recommendations for a position there upon my graduation.

The freedom that came with living away from the church was refreshing, in the lightest of terms. I immersed myself in my studies because I was studying what I wanted to. I took a particular interest in the Western Schism. Something told me the conflict involved a struggle between the *Optio* and the *Iniquus*. If they could not control *De Wil*, control over the Catholic Church would be a worthy consolation prize. But there was no way to confirm my theory, so I kept it to myself.

I still encountered issues with the *Iniquus*, but they were vastly outnumbered by the *Optio* in our Catholic environment. I made friends for the first time in my life, and I learned the value of trusted companions. They helped to keep the *Iniquus* at bay and taught me more about the connection between *De Wil* and those with the gift to feel it.

I saw members of the *Optio* interact with those in need, befriending them, educating them, then taking their leave. I even received a summons from the book on occasion, but my priority was always to keep it safe. I did not know what might happen if I lost *De Wil*, but my gut told me that I did not want to find out.

And yet I did. Another war broke out years later, when I was older, somewhat wiser, and had earned myself a position at the Catholic University teaching history. I was called to enter the Belgian military for the briefest of times. However, I would have preferred to stay at the university. We were not the strongest force in the world and were quickly humbled by the weight of war, but some of us continued to fight.

I was among a large contingent sent to England in 1940. That is where I learned to speak this language.

I met more members of the *Optio* there and, inevitably, some of the *Iniquus* as well.

It was late in the year 1941 that I learned the consequences of losing the book. In the rush and chaos that is war, I had foolishly decided that the book was safe, buried among the possessions I kept beneath my camp bed. Thirty-six years of life, twenty-three of them in possession of *De Wil*, and still a life of limited responsibility had left me spoiled. To be fair, I had a war on my mind, but as the keeper of *De Wil*, the book should have been my foremost priority.

Even when fighting for the same cause, there are still enemies to be found among friends. The Second World War did not cause the *Iniquus* and the *Optio* members to forget the purpose they were born with. I should have been even more responsible.

It was something as small as a surprise drill in the middle of the night that left me careless. Soldiers were the type of men I trusted most, thanks to my French predecessor, but I should not have been so naïve.

Hindsight makes everything so clear, and I should have recognized that the drill was a distraction. As the call rang out and we all rushed to our positions, an *Iniquus* sneaked into my barracks. It was only too easy for him to take *De Wil* once he felt it nearby.

I felt it too. As did several *Optio* members, whose eyes were immediately fixed on me. My first instinct was to run back and catch the thief as soon as possible, but abandoning my post would have taken me even further away from my chances. The punishment for such an act was severe, and while I faced the consequences, the book would be falling ever farther from my grasp. I have never felt so impatient in my life, before or since. The minute we were dismissed, I hurried back, looking for anyone headed in the opposite direction. When that was fruitless, I searched for clues around my bed that I knew would not be there.

I flipped the bed.

I gathered the *Optio*, and I apologized. We searched, but it was a frustrating process. The book called to us, but the *Iniquus* kept it moving.

We knew that something terrible was coming. I could feel so many pages of the book rewriting to compensate for the increasing amount of time that it was lost. It was still sending the message of what had to be done to put God's plan on track, but the *Iniquus* had the hard copy. They had the pages. They could read everything, which no one was truly meant to do. Omniscience is a curse that God keeps to Himself. Father Bediende warned me of that years ago, reading about other people in other places became my obsession.

As always, he had been absolutely correct. For every instruction the book gave, the *Iniquus* could see and counteract it, even those meant for others to act on. Members of the *Optio* and the *Iniquus* must have felt the repercussions worldwide. As if the world was not in enough peril, things were about to get much worse.

It was difficult to hide our intentions from our commanding officers, but honestly, who would accept our story? A book with God's plan written inside that speaks to a particular group of people who can act on it?

How easily would you believe that? There was no time to take the chance. Every spare moment was spent searching the bunks of hundreds of men, but I should have known that the *Iniquus* would not repeat my mistake.

We would have to wait for them to make a mistake of their own, and they inevitably did.

Their mistake was born of selfishness and insensitivity—a common vice among them, which resulted in one of their own betraying them. He found me easily, and we wasted no time reclaiming the book, but not without a fight.

There was a skirmish, which I expected, but what I did not expect was that one of the *Iniquus* would pull his gun on us once I had wrestled *De Wil* from him. Fortunately, our heads were clearer with the book back in my possession, as were our assignments. In an action that the book must have directed, one of the *Optio* tackled the armed man as he fired his gun.

A cry rang out, and it was mine. I had been shot in the foot, and all the British soldiers complimented me on what they called my "blighty" wound. For me, the fighting was over, the book was found, and all was well.

However, nothing is so easy, and we were still too late. No sooner had I breathed a sigh of relief than the news came in of an attack on America that set a new fire to the war. That was early December 1941.

From then on, I learned the value of a buttoned inside pocket and kept the book safely within one at all times.

It was a lesson learned too late I am afraid. Just because the book was restored to its rightful keeper did not mean that the damage was undone. In fact, the pages became so full in the years that followed that one could not hope to read them all. As soon as the last page was turned, the others would be full again with new assignments. Even I was tasked more than ever in an effort to mend what had been torn.

Now, that is not to say that every cataclysmic event between then and now was due to my poor performance; though there are more than I have the humility to admit, I learned a valuable lesson from them.

When I was discharged, and well enough, I returned to Hooge because the book called me there. It did not warn me, however, of what I was to find.

My sister married and had a family, but the old friend and teacher I was eager to visit could only meet me as a name written in polished stone. No battle had taken him. The murderer, in this case, was simply time.

Yet, it was this moment that inspired me. Kneeling in the rain-soaked earth before a man who had been twice a father to me, I suddenly knew why he placed me where he was, why he taught me so persistently. The book needed to be kept safe, and there was only one place where I would be able to live in peace while protecting it. Father Bediende had realized it immediately, and he had tried to prepare me for it.

I began my journey to Rome. By this time, I had reached the age of forty, but the process in Rome would not be a quick one. *De Wil* told me that I needed to find a position in the Vatican, which would require effort since I was not a priest. So, I returned to Leuven to continue my work and await an opportunity that I knew God would provide through *De Wil's* pages.

All those years later, I still felt as restless as when Father Bediende and I had first started. The only exception was that this time, I knew what was at stake. That made the process all the more grueling.

Suddenly, I was grateful for those years spent in the church and the schooling I had received.

Of course, it became evident that these things were not a coincidence.

In my time at the university, the *Iniquus* continued to seek me out, and they found me often enough. Still, I was creative with my methods of hiding *De Wil*. I buried it, kept it in deposit boxes, even put it within the pages of larger books in my library. So, when I found myself in the presence of *Iniquus* members, the only thing they could hope to gain was information. Well, they certainly were not going to get it.

As I took increasingly drastic measures in hiding the book, the *Iniquus* made more extraordinary efforts to oppose me. In the most extreme case, I found myself cornered on a back street, surrounded by five men.

They spoke to me at first, trying to coax a middle-aged man into joining them. It was all very similar to my childhood, only the roles were reversed. They were young. I was old enough to have been a father to any one of them. They thought me old, crippled, and foolish, but I can promise I was not so old in either mind or body. I had just finished military service, and I had a walking cane at my disposal now.

Knives were pulled, but I had tasted war twice and, though I was now a God-fearing man, the boy from Hooge still lingered. I am a guardian, my friend, not a saint. That is a calling left to better people than myself. However, five against one is still not a fair fight. I could only do what I was capable of, and that would never be enough.

By this time, I was known well enough that the shout of my voice drew attention. Whether this time it was the attention of the *Optio* or fellow members of university staff, I might never know, but *De Wil* was just as safe hidden beneath the mattress of my hospital bed for a few nights. I was grateful for any form of security I could find until I reached my ultimate goal.

I will not mislead you and say that no strings were pulled on my behalf to afford me the position in the middle staff of the Vatican archives some years later when the dust of war finally began to settle in Italy. But the calling of a faithful man is to live in the service and footsteps of the Lord. Is that not what I have done? If it were not meant to be, then *De Wil* would have spoken against it, and it has not.

I was sent by my university to research the Great Schism with the support of my church. My diligence and commitment to my research were noticed over a period of time, and I was asked to collaborate with the staff on internal archive projects. This opportunity thrilled me and led to my placement on the staff several years later.

I have earned my position, and, to be honest, few others know the truth behind who I am, save for the Vatican Archivist. That was another fortunate turn of events.

For my entire duration at the Vatican, *De Wil* has remained a hidden secret, an ancient, blank tome to all who view it without the calling to it. It has been considered a harmless, empty piece of history.

Finally, I slept soundly at night. But times, once again, are changing quickly, and we are welcoming an age of free information. I cannot tell you how wonderful it is that the wall of separation between our wisdom and God's people is being torn down.

God has nothing to hide from His people. That is precisely why the *Optio* are sent out to the world, and *De Wil* is kept by a single man—to educate people without overwhelming them. Some say knowledge is power, and they are correct enough, but too much knowledge is panic, my friend. If everyone could read *De Wil* at their leisure, they would not believe that their lives were theirs to live as they choose. That is unfair to them.

This is why *De Wil* must be held in the hands of only one person. To most, it would be an uninteresting blank book, but to those who can read its contents, it is a prize and potentially a weapon. The book must be moved once again.

And that is why it summoned you here today. I know you have felt it, so I will not bore you with redundant talk of destiny. You have lived the proof you need every time you have followed a gut instinct to help someone. Perhaps you were never told just how this knowledge came to you, but now you have, my friend, and it is time to act.

I pass the responsibility for the book on to you, as *De Wil* has instructed me to do.

I know you have questions, and there will be help. I would promise my support to you, but I feel that will not be an option for much longer.

∾

KristaLyn is an internationally bestselling author, multi-certified metaphysical practitioner, and psychic mentor who helps people attract the lives they want to live aligned with astrology and their Divine timing.

She has published more than a dozen books in both fiction and nonfiction, all with empowering themes of being your own hero and serving the world through your unique talents and gifts, which she knows everyone is born with. KristaLyn lives in a treehouse in Pennsylvania with her husband and corgis, Jack and Zelda, and cooperates with her family to help revitalize the Coal Region of Pennsylvania to a new, sustainable glory. Website: www.KristaLynAVetovich.com *Email:* info@KristaLynAVetovich.com *Social Media Handle:* @TheRealKristaLyn

SHADOW REELS
SUZANNE WYLES

My eyes deceive me. And my ears. I think I remember the time when the world was different. Still, our memories are only hours old—unreliable at best and treasonous at worst.

If you can find them, there are books that speak of such a time when the line between reality and fiction was not blurred.

These lines met for me two years ago, when the world of the old and the world of the new came together on my seventeenth birthday in the guise of presents.

My best, and admittedly only, friend Marie gave me the *new*.

She'd been working on an engrossing software that compiled video and audio footage of our favorite celebrities. Then she could make them do and say anything she wanted.

When I jumped into that holo-skin and combined Marie's technology with my natural story-telling, we were able to create what we called "Shadow Reels". They were fake stories but looked like an actual recording. We replayed the video over and over again.

Under cover of darkness after Marie left, my GiGi gifted me the *past*. She had been my support system since my mom disappeared. She opened up the holo-screen that took up the majority of our living room and revealed a space I didn't even know existed. Her back room was devoid of all technology, even lights. It was here where she showed me her deepest secret—and most dangerous treasure.

Lining the walls, stacked on shelves from floor to ceiling, every surface was covered in paper: books, magazines, notebooks, random pages. I remember running my hands along it, the texture reaching back at me, grabbing my fingers, damp with perspiration.

When I demanded answers, GiGi merely smiled and waved away any warnings. She'd had these for half a century since her mother passed them down to her—never mind the Cooperative's tightening regulations on the types and quantities of old literature a single person could own.

She handed me a single empty journal to add my voice to her collected works of the thousands of people who came before me.

I pushed aside the caution that had been distilled in me and let curiosity take over. I lost myself in the old as the new gained a life of its own.

Those weeks after my birthday were chaotic. The recording of our Shadow Reels hit the Bleeding Edge Column, and it seemed like everyone in the world saw it. Marie and I were soon being wooed by the most influential corporation in the world—The Cooperative.

My journal entries from this time were half-finished, full of exclamation points and quotes from forgotten authors.

The Co-Op funded expensive trips to their headquarters, fancy business galas where they sent us on a shopping spree—after all, I'd never even had a prom dress, much less a cocktail dress. It was here we were introduced as "the innovative ladies behind that sensational new app," and they paraded us around conferences and meetings. It was easy to ignore the feeling of being a zoo animal when we were surrounded by opulence. How could we say no to this amazing opportunity?

We couldn't.

The Cooperative bought Marie's Shadow Reels software and hired her to make it better. I was hired for Ideation—idea creation. The Co-Op was never creative with names, maybe why they wanted me.

KASSANDRA. My name in bold platinum marked my workstation, one floor separating Marie and me. Every week was something new and interesting. The Co-Op would give me a brief where I would pretend to be someone new, usually a politician or celebrity, and write their thoughts on a particular subject.

And I was good at it. Flexing my writing and research muscles never felt so freeing. As long as I hit their talking points, the rest was my invention.

Shadow Reels ⌒ Suzanne Wyles

One week, I was the new president of North Korea, explaining my disdain for holo-screen technology. The next, I was the latest Disney star urging people to buy the Co-Op's latest and greatest must-haves.

It was hard managing the creative output demanded by the Cooperative as well as my personal writing and reading pursuits. Anne Frank, Frida Kahlo, and Da Vinci filled my mind and influenced my writing.

I spent the next year reading and praying the old knowledge—new to my mind—didn't show on my face. My friend spent her year also growing her technological ability, surpassing many supposed experts.

I was keeping daily entries and filled my second journal when I saw it—my words coming out of the mouth of a politician on the holo-screen.

Marie and I watched in silence, full of knowledge, empty of action.

It happened, again and again. My words and Marie's faces sparking fury, hope, love, and fear. We were spectacular at our jobs.

My GiGi noticed, as she always had a talent for such, my introspection. She didn't ask though; she only handed me a pen and another empty journal. The pen was a vintage ballpoint that has a dent in the ball part so every time I wrote a vowel, it would skip in the ink. I poured invasive, un-cooperative thoughts out by the page.

The Co-Op's briefs got more specific and more time-sensitive. My research e-notes were filled with upper-class politicians, pop-culture sensations, and relevant nobodies brought to light by virality. They paid me well for the reality I was weaving. I felt like a goddess; as soon as I spoke, it became so.

Marie's software was above reproach. She was even trying to come up with a way to do it live. She said it involved a lot of prep work, but once she got everything right, it could be done.

The hundredth broadcast of our work was being aired nation-wide when I decided I needed a break. I sent GiGi a holo-message that I was on my way, turned off my work station, and went home for the first time in months.

The door to the apartment was open.

The candles GiGi always left burning had drowned in wax. Her carefully tended plants were long and wilted. The kitchen light flickered as it did when it was left on for too long.

25 Servings of SOOP

And the door to the back room behind the holo-screen was ajar.

I was surrounded only by blank walls and a lingering musty book smell.

Naturally, I lied through my teeth when interrogated by the Co-Op and neighbors. Of course, I'd never seen the backroom nor the contents before. And she must have been very uncooperative indeed to have brought such vitriol into the house. Cooperative People had come, and the neighbors hadn't seen her since, good riddance. What kind of woman would hold onto such volatile material unless she planned to do something unspeakable with it?

I felt the eyes of the Co-op scrutinize my every move. I only dared to open my journal in the darkest recesses of my closet, a single candle for light. Clothes were easily replaceable if scorched by my words.

Marie whispered to me in the dark too, when we stole time away from the Co-op. Hers was full of terror and caution. We vowed to stay together no matter what.

The Co-op demanded more, better from us. No one was untouchable. The CEOs of other companies, the politician lobbying for governmental oversight, the whistleblower going viral. The Cooperative Megacorp transformed itself into a world-dominating empire with nothing and no one standing in their way.

My journal took on a more structured format. I began talking directly to the people rather than myself. Pleas for change, for education, for old knowledge spilled out from my ballpoint. My words were sharp, demanding, angry. Marie looked them over, again and again, her subtle code writing, enhancing, and placing empathy into it.

Cooperative Day was fast approaching and their New Year's party seemed insignificant compared to the height of the Co-Op pride in February.

It was an honor to be even invited to the New Year's Gala. The week before demanded rigorous preparation, appointments, women eradicating any blemish that dared be seen under their sharp tools. The day of was akin to being attacked by waves of vultures picking at specific parts of you until they deemed perfection.

And I was. Or as close to it as I could get in this lifetime. Marie, however, was brilliance incarnate. We descended into the gala together hand-in-hand.

The night devolved in concurrence with the number of drinks we consumed. The lights were a little too bright, the people a little too pretty, the music a little too pitchy.

Marie's laugh brought me back to reality. She was holding onto the edge of a table and the overly padded shoulder of the head of her department for dear life. The department head was trying to extricate herself from Marie's plan to improve the Co-Op and Shadow Reels.

Before I could dislodge her, Marie had loudly toasted to the Co-Op and their ever-changing reality and drank deeply. I apologized and swept us into a Co-Op limo, ringing in the New Year by hovering over the toilet in my house.

The invitation to the Cooperative Day Conference and a time slot to speak in front of the entire company arrived the next day. The Co-Op values the thoughts of the innovative ladies behind the revolutionary technology of Shadow Reels.

We spent that day planning, writing, and editing our speech. It would be ready. We would be ready. No longer would we stand idly by or actively by while the Co-Op rewrote reality.

And my reality was hard enough to keep track of, between overanalyzing the speech and continuing to put out content for the Co-Op; it took me a week to realize I hadn't seen Marie since the first of the year. When asked, her head of department, no longer endowed with overly padded shoulders, just shrugged and said the Co-Op had her working at another site.

Her holo either wasn't connected, or she was just ignoring me, something she'd never done in our nineteen-year relationship.

The weeks and my anxiety went into overdrive. My journal was full of unfinished, poorly thought-out thoughts. I curled up in the closet, comforted only by my candle and Marie's old sweatshirt, and waited for Cooperative Day.

As suddenly as she had vanished, Marie reappeared in my workspace on the eve of the conference. When asked, no longer endowed with a hangover, she just shrugged and said the Co-Op had had her working at another site. But she was excited and ready for tomorrow, just like we planned.

Oddly enough, my nerves disappeared that morning, replaced with determination. I lit GiGi's candle and took Marie's hand.

The conference was a blur of holo-screens, applause, and alcohol, which we successfully evaded. And then it was time.

Marie dropped my hand and sat in the front row while I ascended onto the stage.

I stood above the crowd, knowing my rousing speech was incorruptible, written by my own hand on the paper before me.

I began and watched my face on the screen projected above the audience in real time.

My lips moved, and my voice boomed out, praising the good of the Co-Op.

My scream reached only the Cooperative People in the first row, who paid me no mind.

∽

Suzanne Wyles is a twenty-something woman who is hell-bent on being a "doer" and not a "talker." She is part of many writing communities and has enrolled in several nationally recognized writing workshops. She has five college degrees and has traveled to five continents thus far. Her travel has exposed her to this amazing, diverse world and that world to her. Rose-colored glasses tangle with her entrepreneurial mind that created three businesses and countless worlds in her writing. Continuing to push the boundaries of story-telling and her own creativity is what she will always strive for.